Further adventures of Simon and Chester:

Simon AND Chester
Super Sleepover!
Cale Atkinson

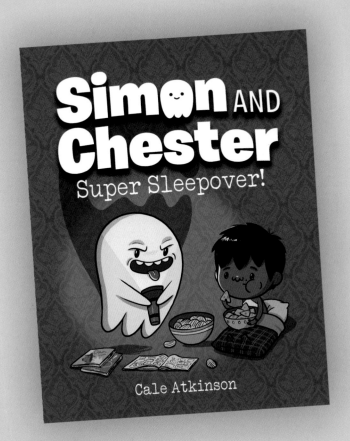

Dedicated to Sam, for believing
in a ghost named Simon

Paperback edition published by Tundra Books, 2022

Text and illustrations copyright © 2021 by Cale Atkinson

Tundra Books, an imprint of Penguin Random House Canada Young Readers,
a division of Penguin Random House of Canada Limited

Library and Archives Canada Cataloguing in Publication

Title: Super detectives / Cale Atkinson.
Names: Atkinson, Cale, author, illustrator.
Description: Series statement: Simon and Chester
Identifiers: Canadiana 20200416766 | ISBN 9780735267640 (softcover)
Subjects: LCGFT: Graphic novels.
Classification: LCC PN6733.A85 S87 2022 | DDC j741.5/971—dc23

Published simultaneously in the United States of America by Tundra Books of Northern
New York, an imprint of Penguin Random House Canada Young Readers, a division of
Penguin Random House of Canada Limited

Library of Congress Control Number: 2020933320

Edited by Samantha Swenson
Designed by John Martz
This book was rendered in ectoplasm, pug fur and Photoshop.
The text was set in Silver Age BB.

Printed in China

www.penguinrandomhouse.ca

1   2   3   4   5   26   25   24   23   22

tundra | Penguin
Random House
TUNDRA BOOKS

Simon AND Chester

Super Detectives!

by Cale Atkinson

tundra

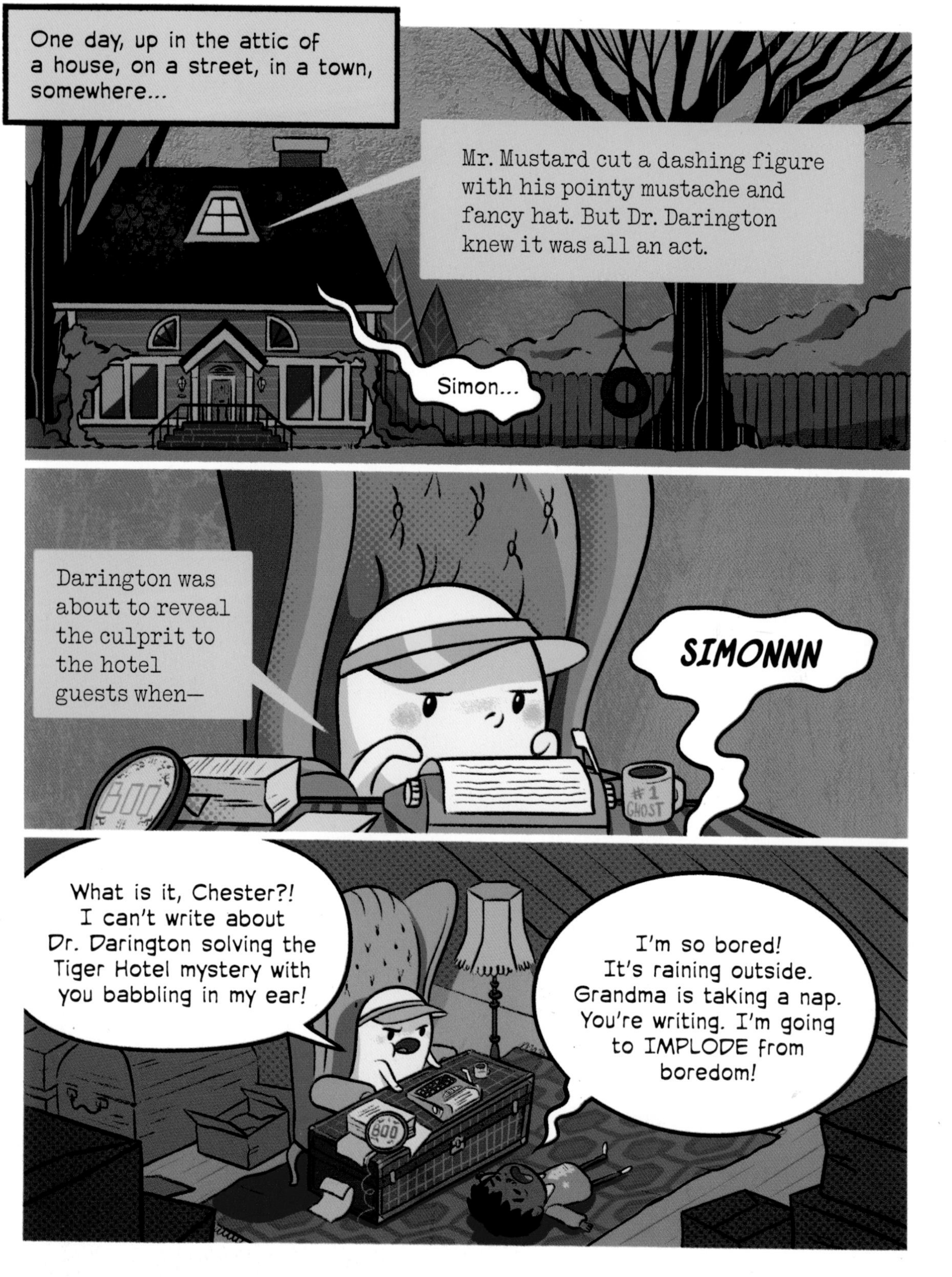
One day, up in the attic of a house, on a street, in a town, somewhere...
Mr. Mustard cut a dashing figure with his pointy mustache and fancy hat. But Dr. Darington knew it was all an act.
Simon...
Darington was about to reveal the culprit to the hotel guests when—
SIMONNN
BOO
#1 GHOST
What is it, Chester?! I can't write about Dr. Darington solving the Tiger Hotel mystery with you babbling in my ear!
I'm so bored! It's raining outside. Grandma is taking a nap. You're writing. I'm going to IMPLODE from boredom!
BOO

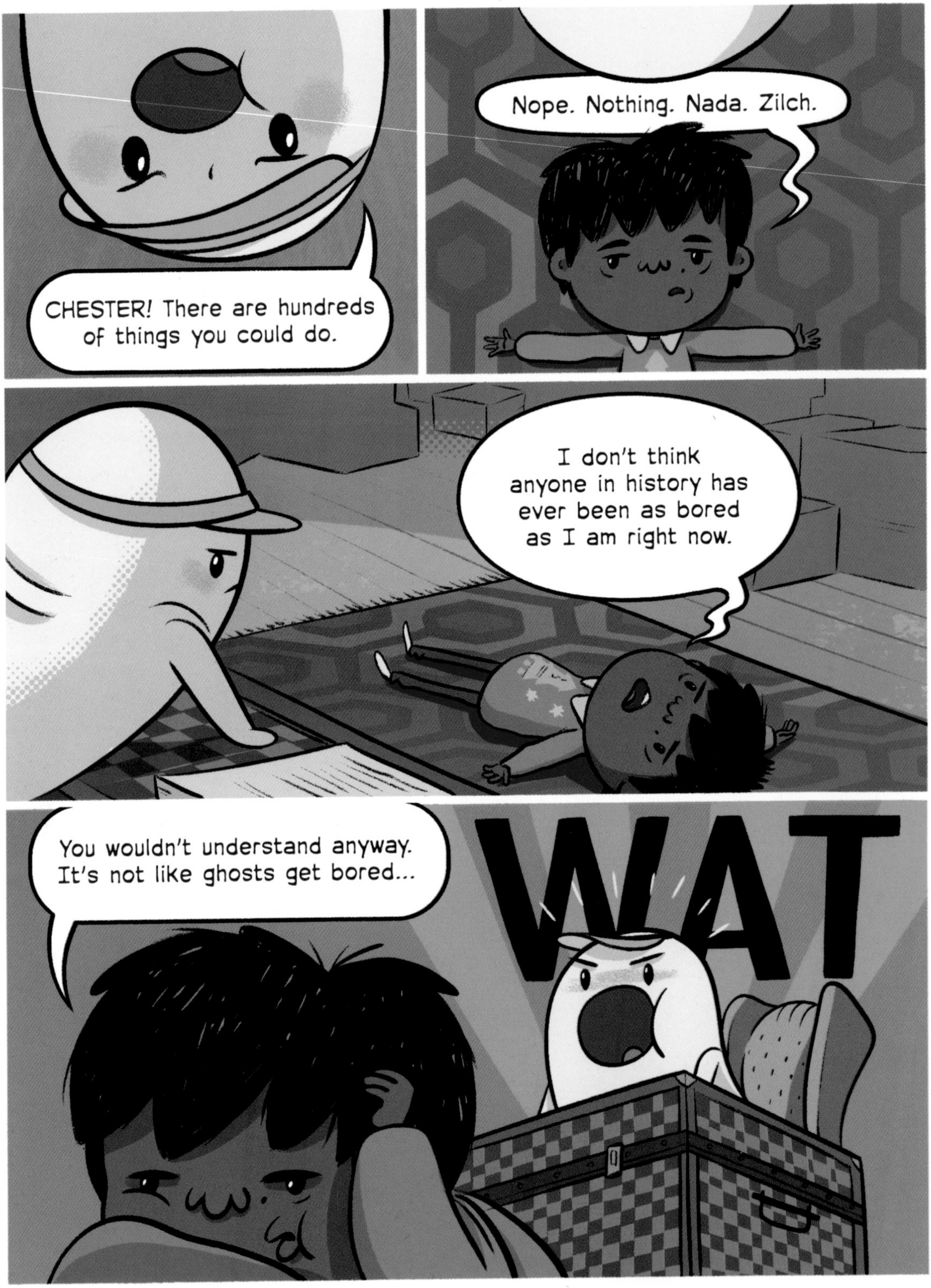
CHESTER! There are hundreds of things you could do.
Nope. Nothing. Nada. Zilch.
I don't think anyone in history has ever been as bored as I am right now.
You wouldn't understand anyway. It's not like ghosts get bored...
WAT

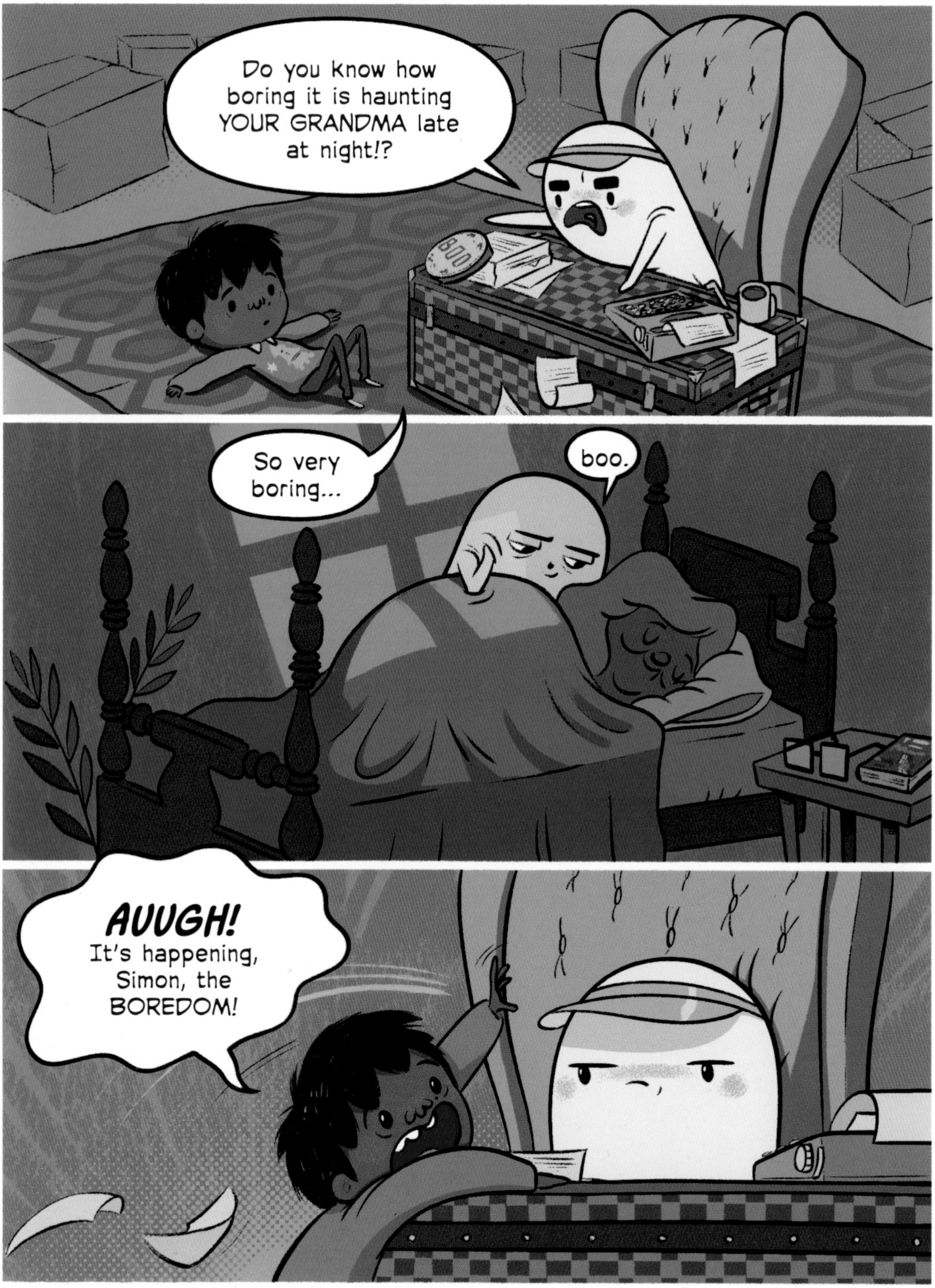
Do you know how boring it is haunting YOUR GRANDMA late at night!?
BOO
So very boring...
boo.
AUUGH!
It's happening, Simon, the BOREDOM!

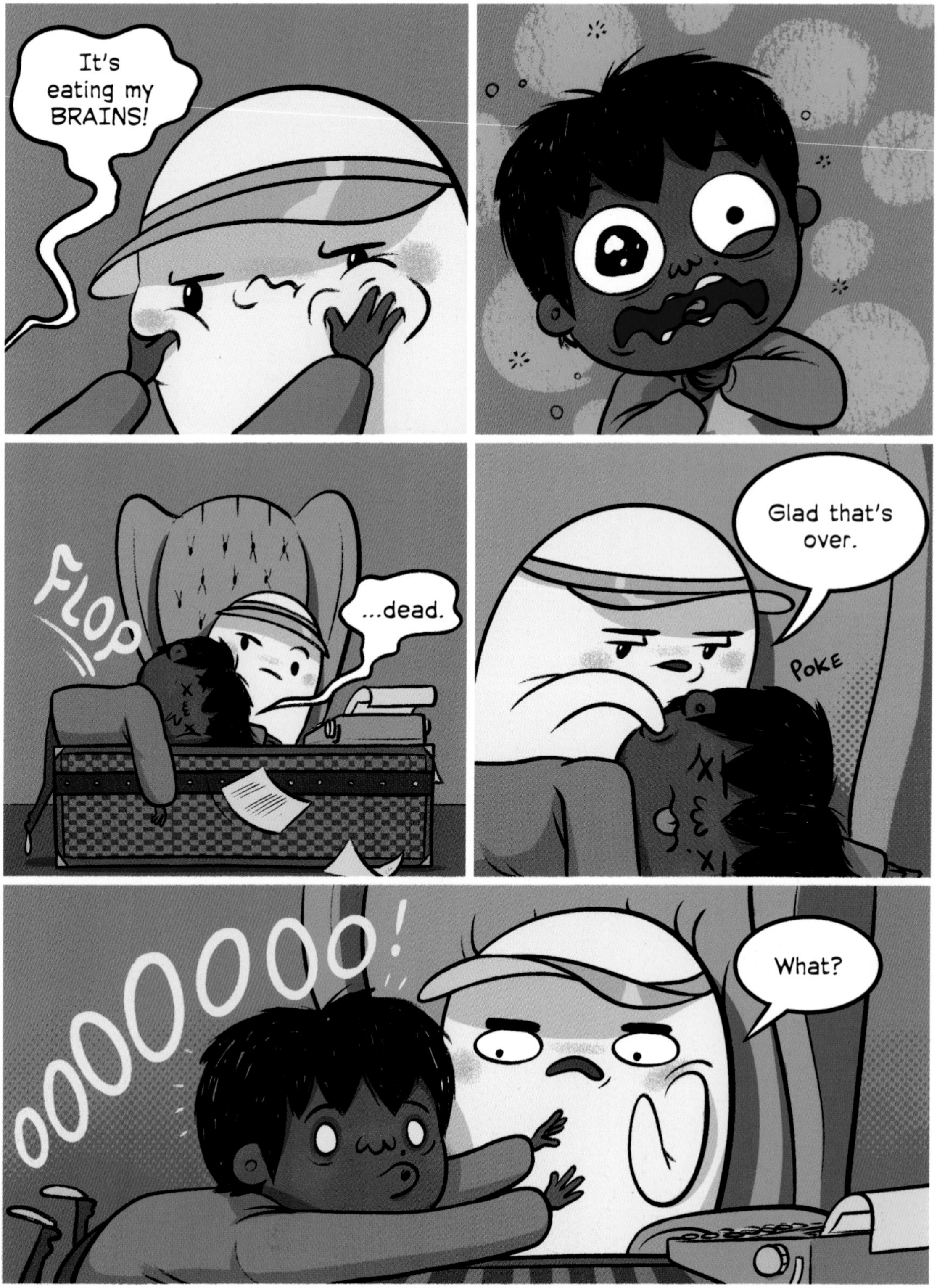
It's eating my BRAINS!
FLOP
...dead.
Glad that's over.
POKE
OOOOOOOO!
What?

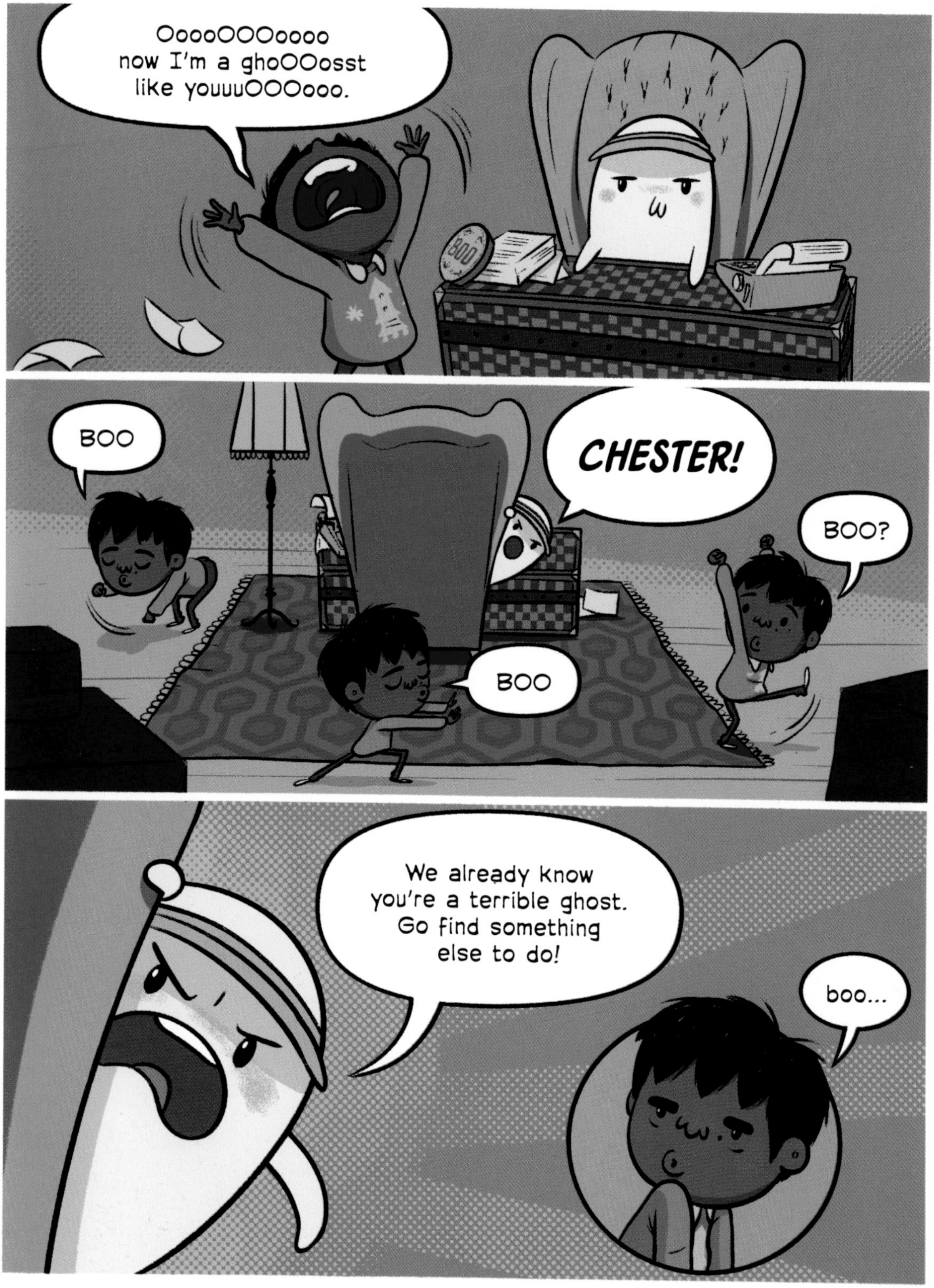
OoooOOOoooo
now I'm a ghoOOosst
like youuuOOOooo.
BOO
CHESTER!
BOO?
BOO
We already know
you're a terrible ghost.
Go find something
else to do!
boo...

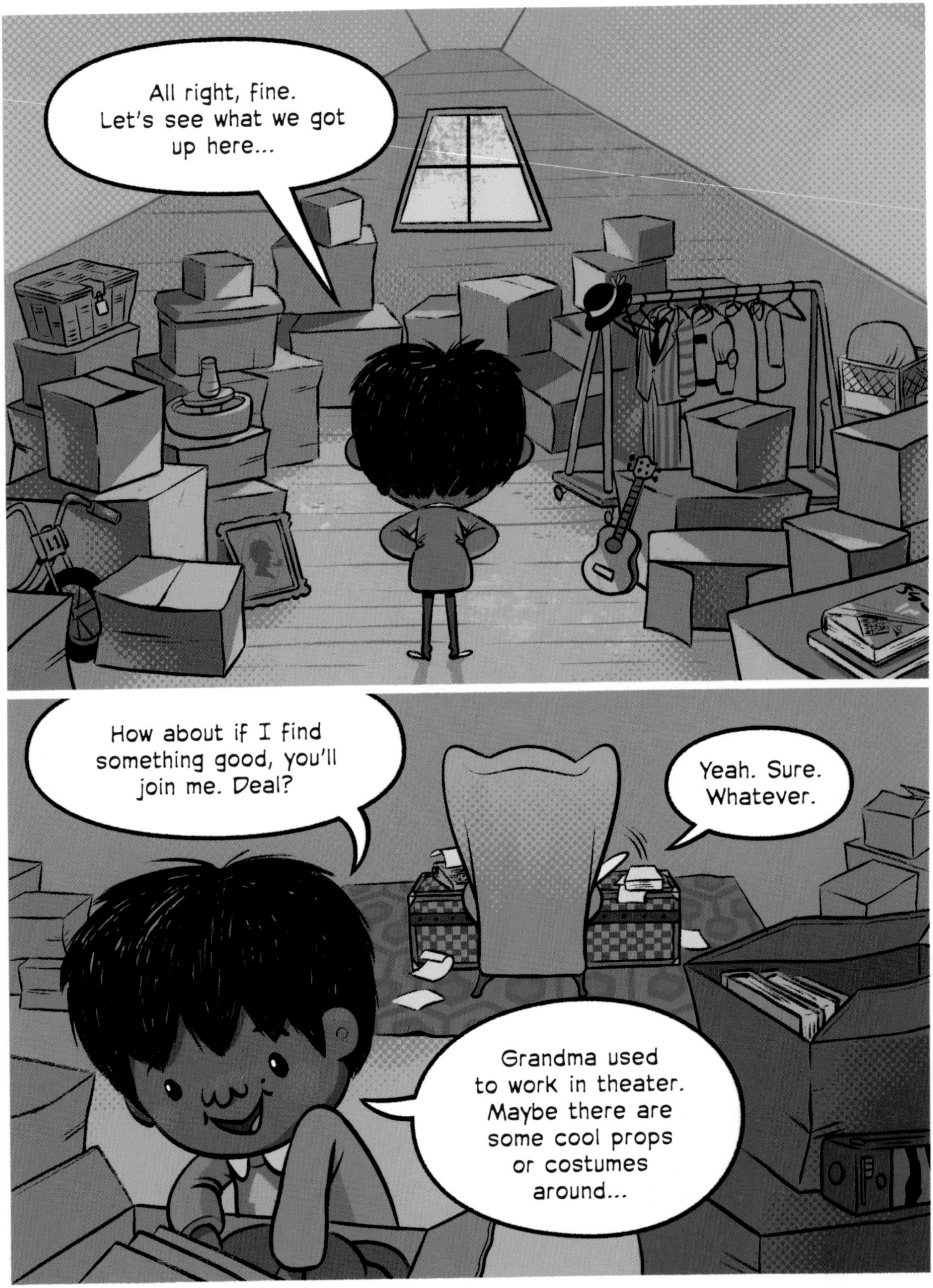
All right, fine. Let's see what we got up here...
How about if I find something good, you'll join me. Deal?
Yeah. Sure. Whatever.
Grandma used to work in theater. Maybe there are some cool props or costumes around...

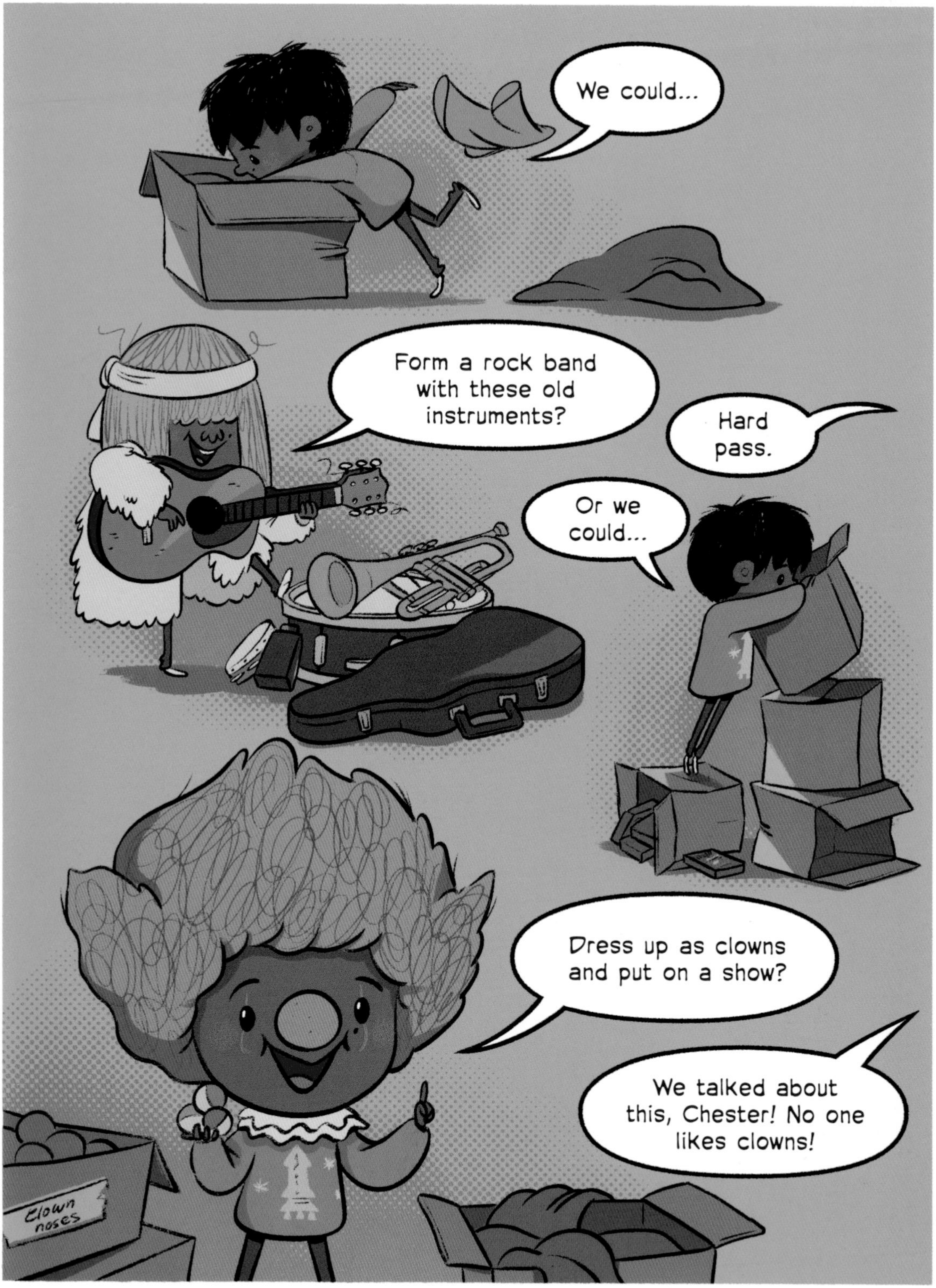
We could...
Form a rock band with these old instruments?
Hard pass.
Or we could...
Dress up as clowns and put on a show?
We talked about this, Chester! No one likes clowns!
Clown noses

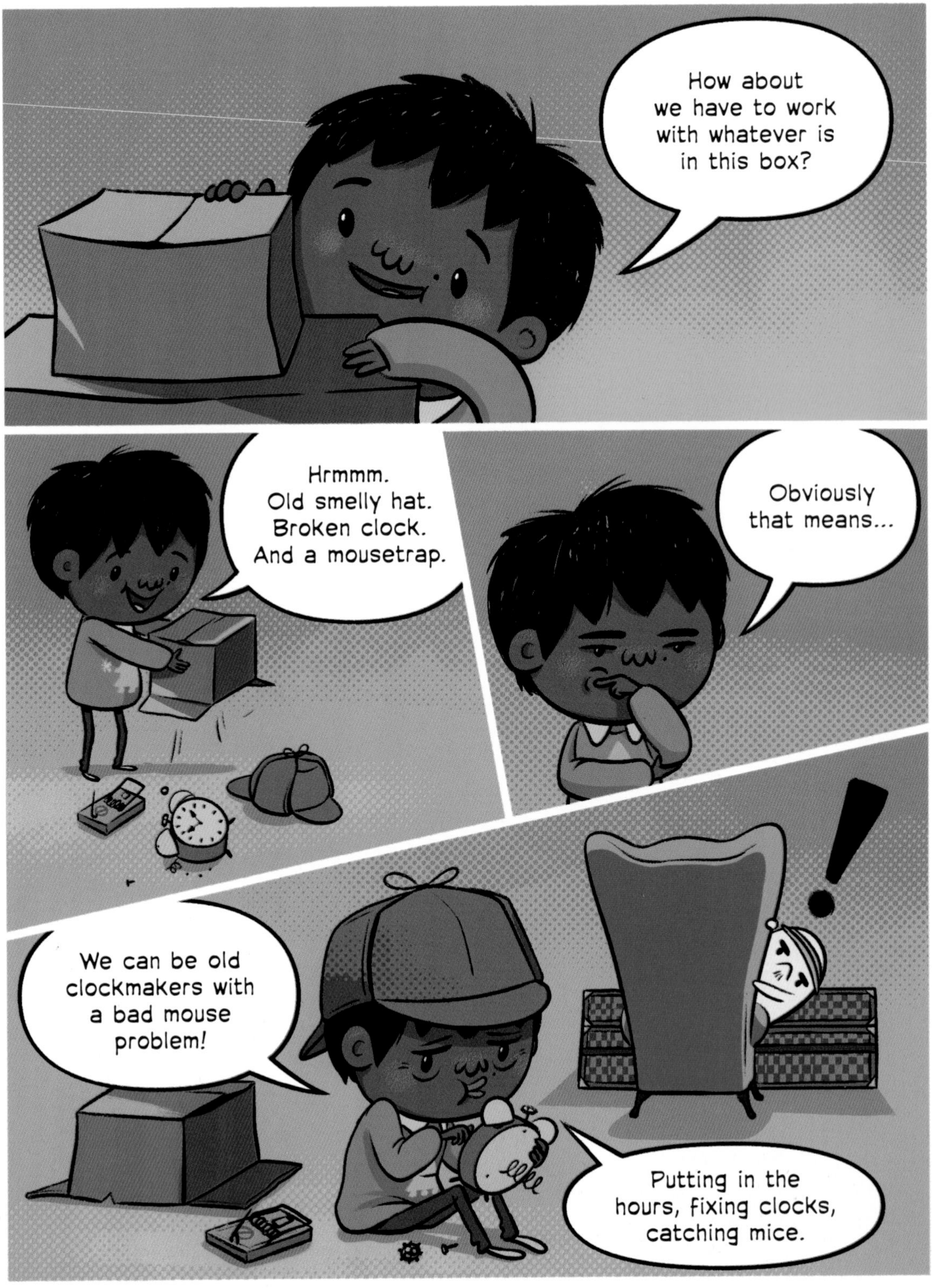
How about we have to work with whatever is in this box?
Hrmmm. Old smelly hat. Broken clock. And a mousetrap.
Obviously that means...
We can be old clockmakers with a bad mouse problem!
Putting in the hours, fixing clocks, catching mice.

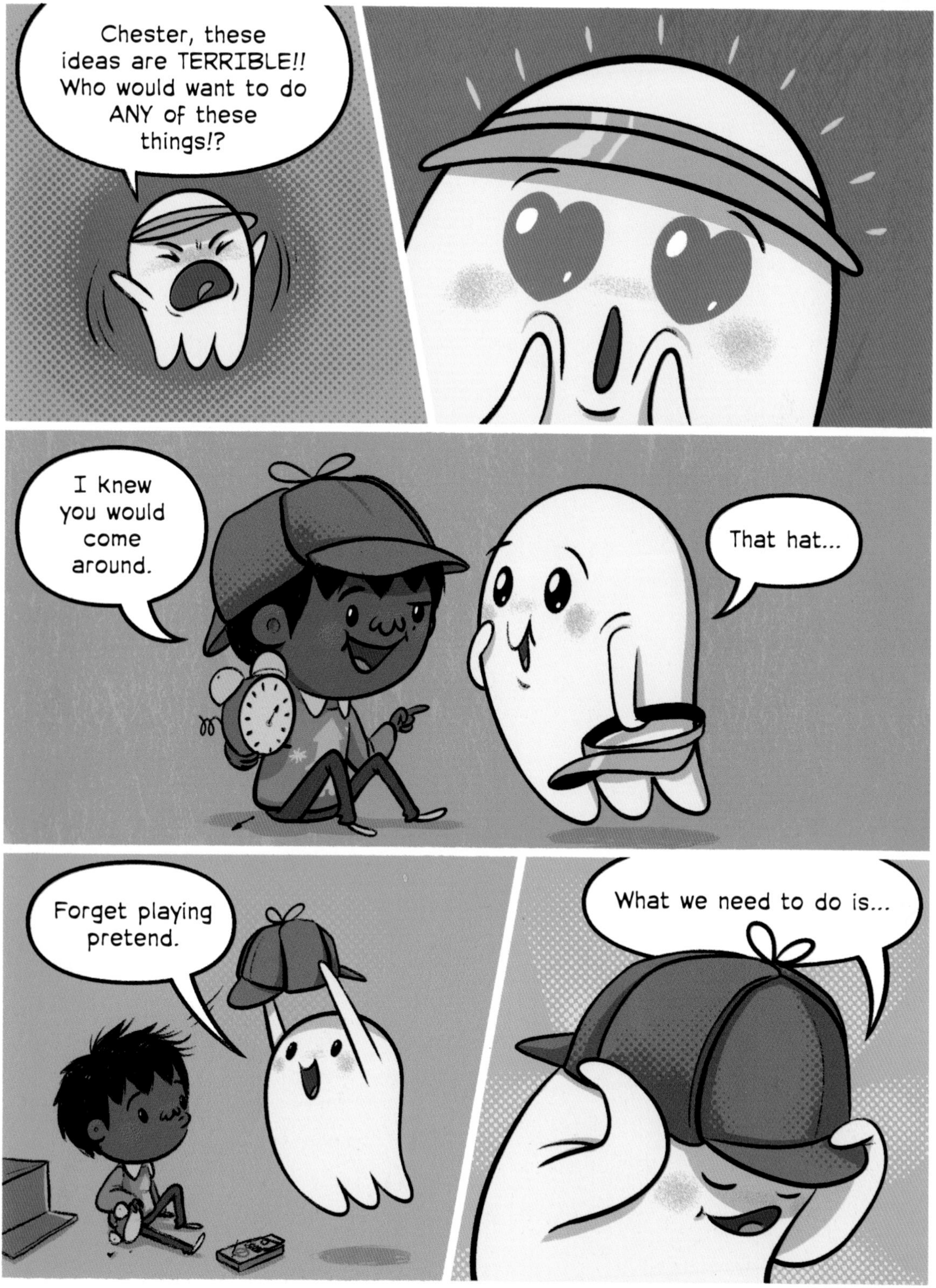
Chester, these ideas are TERRIBLE!! Who would want to do ANY of these things!?
I knew you would come around.
That hat...
Forget playing pretend.
What we need to do is...

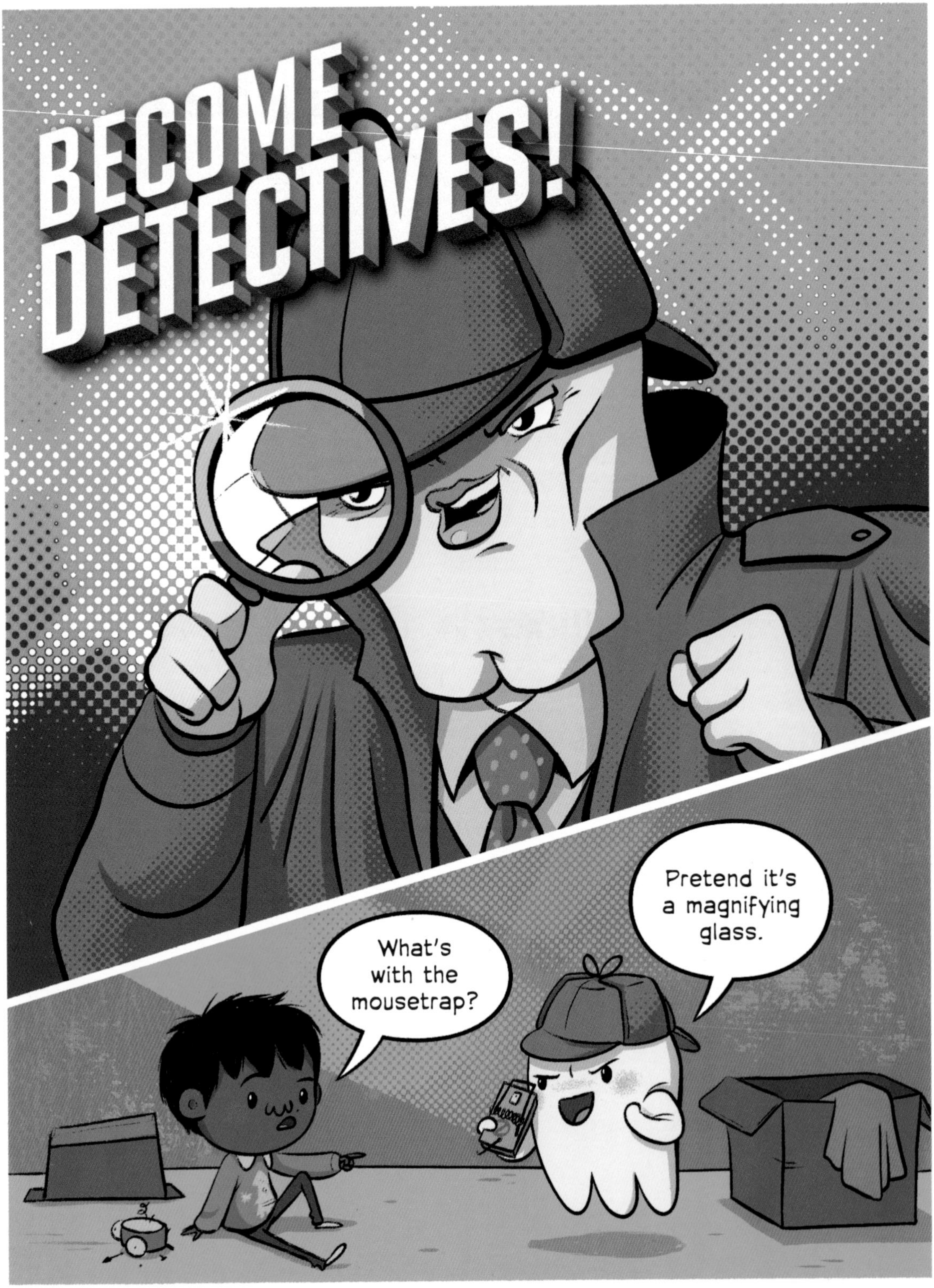
BECOME DETECTIVES!
What's with the mousetrap?
Pretend it's a magnifying glass.

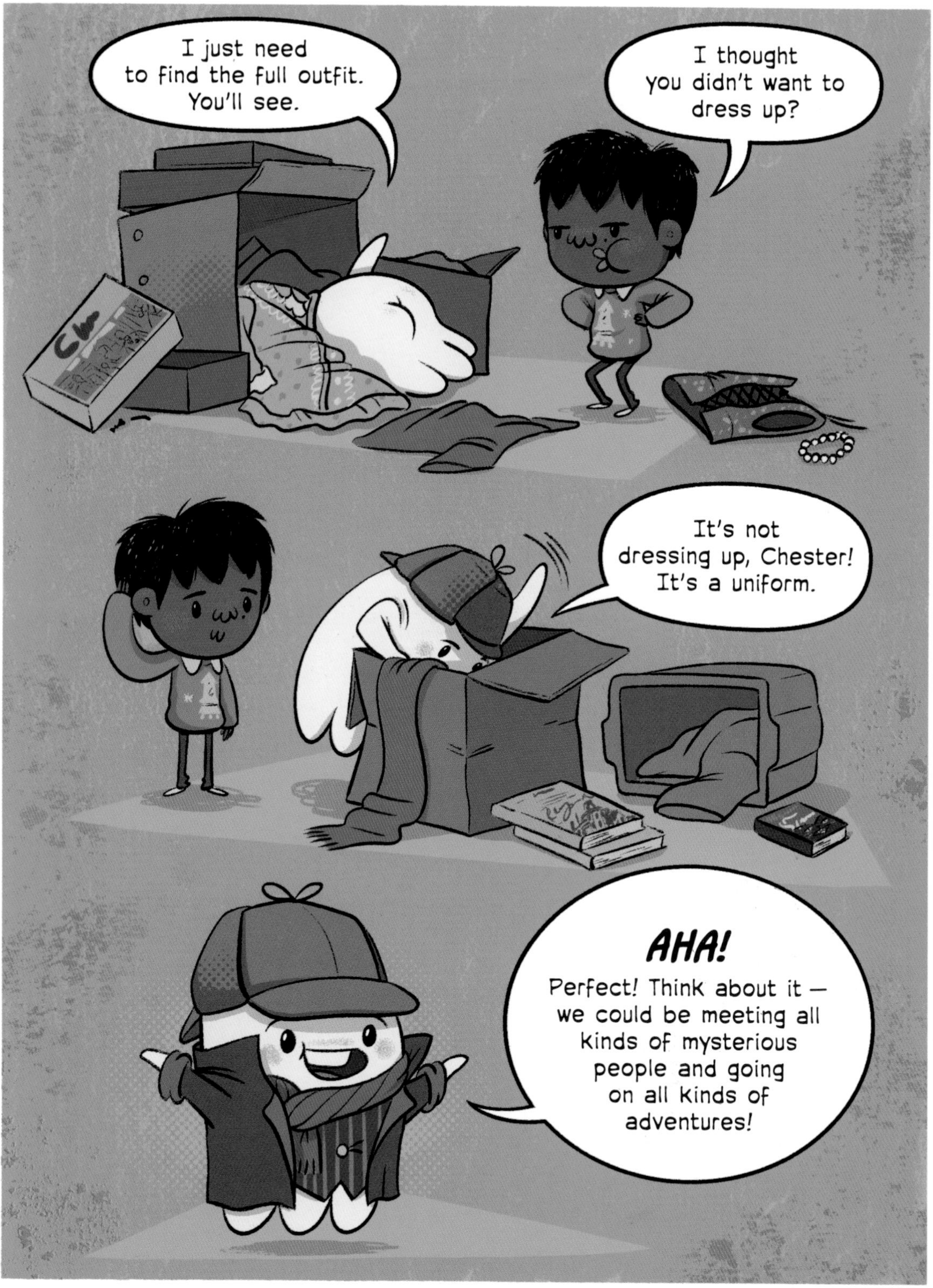
I just need to find the full outfit. You'll see.
I thought you didn't want to dress up?
It's not dressing up, Chester! It's a uniform.
AHA!
Perfect! Think about it — we could be meeting all kinds of mysterious people and going on all kinds of adventures!

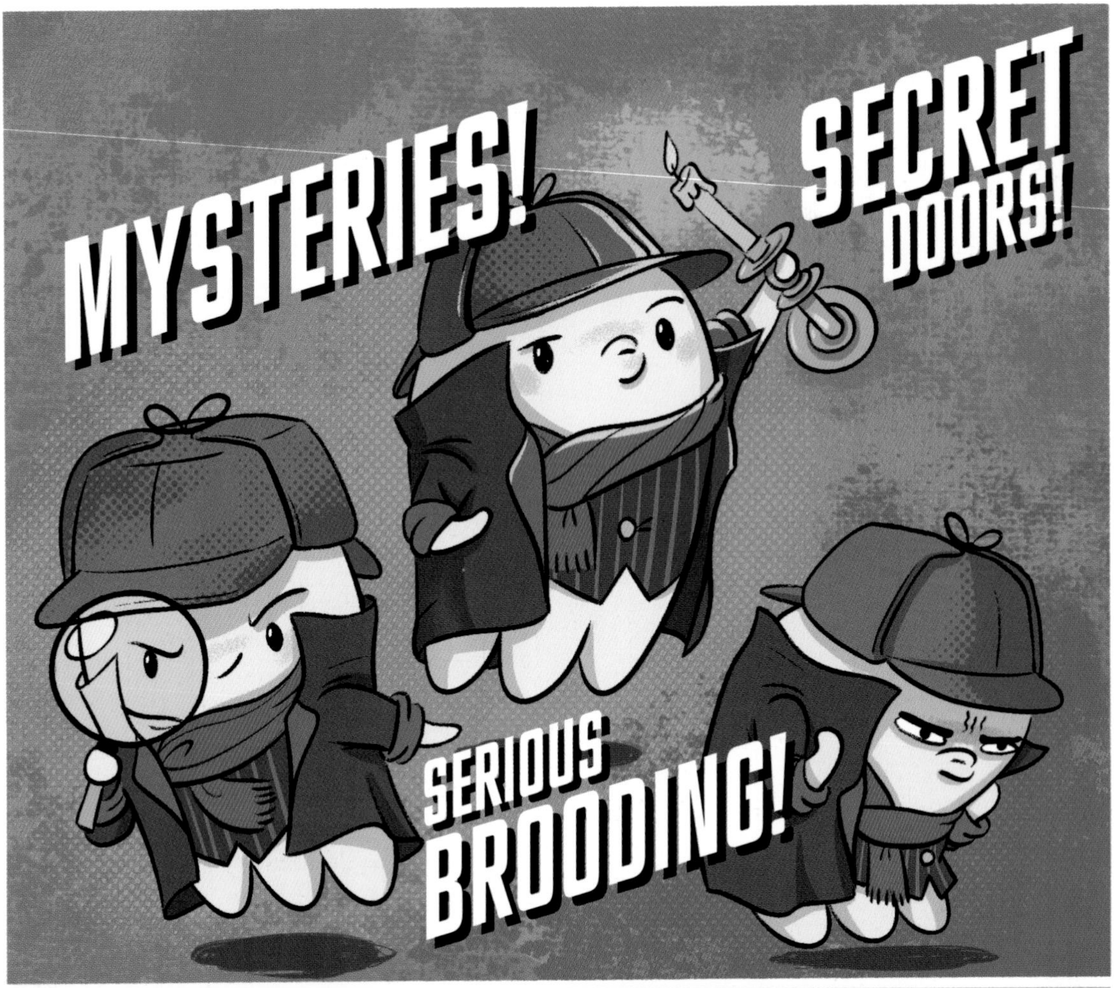
MYSTERIES!
SECRET DOORS!!
SERIOUS BROODING!

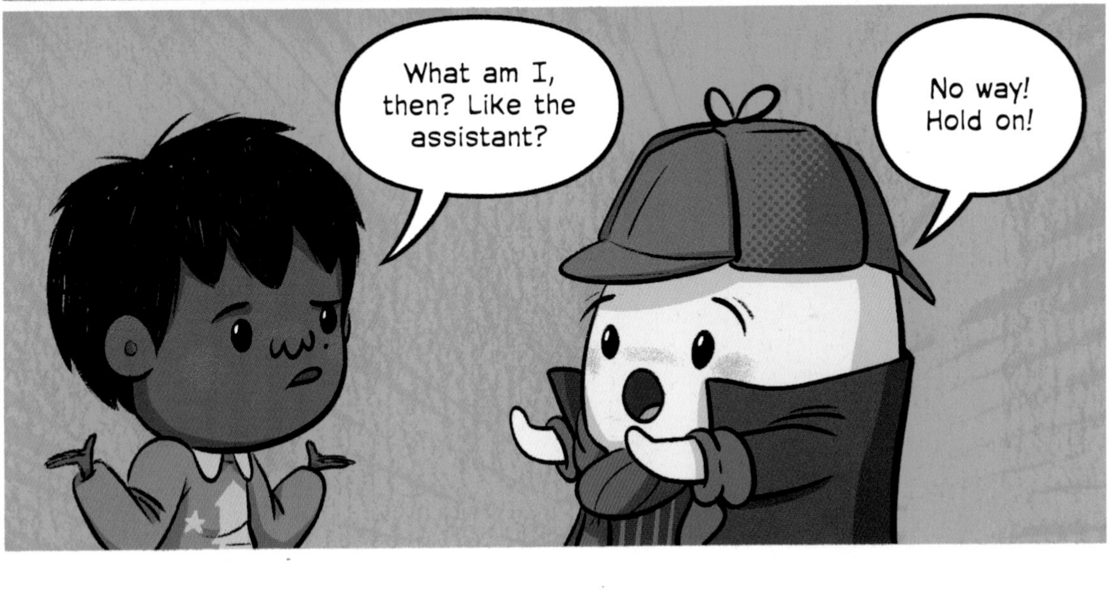
What am I, then? Like the assistant?
No way! Hold on!

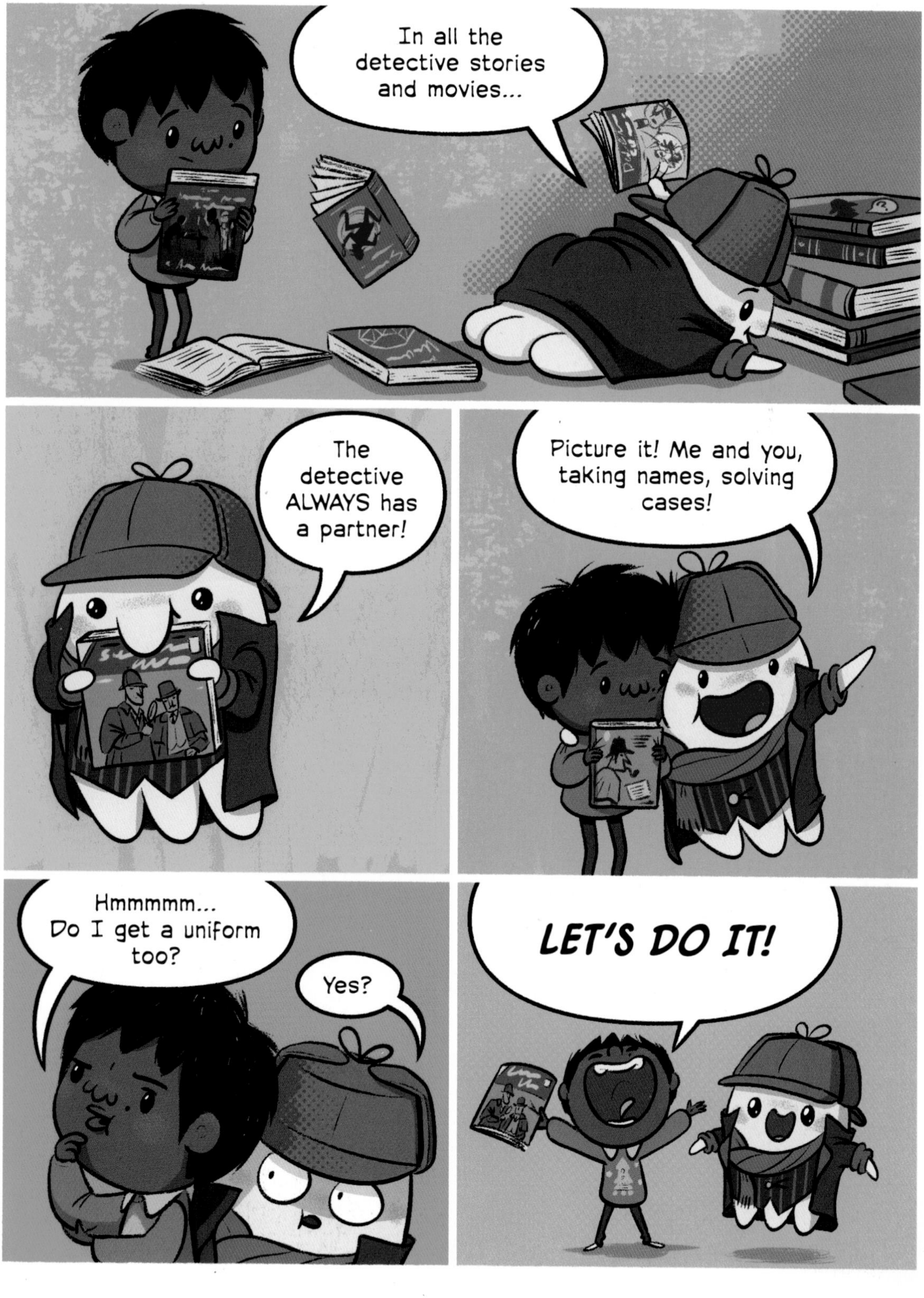
In all the detective stories and movies...
The detective ALWAYS has a partner!
Picture it! Me and you, taking names, solving cases!
Hmmmmm... Do I get a uniform too?
Yes?
LET'S DO IT!

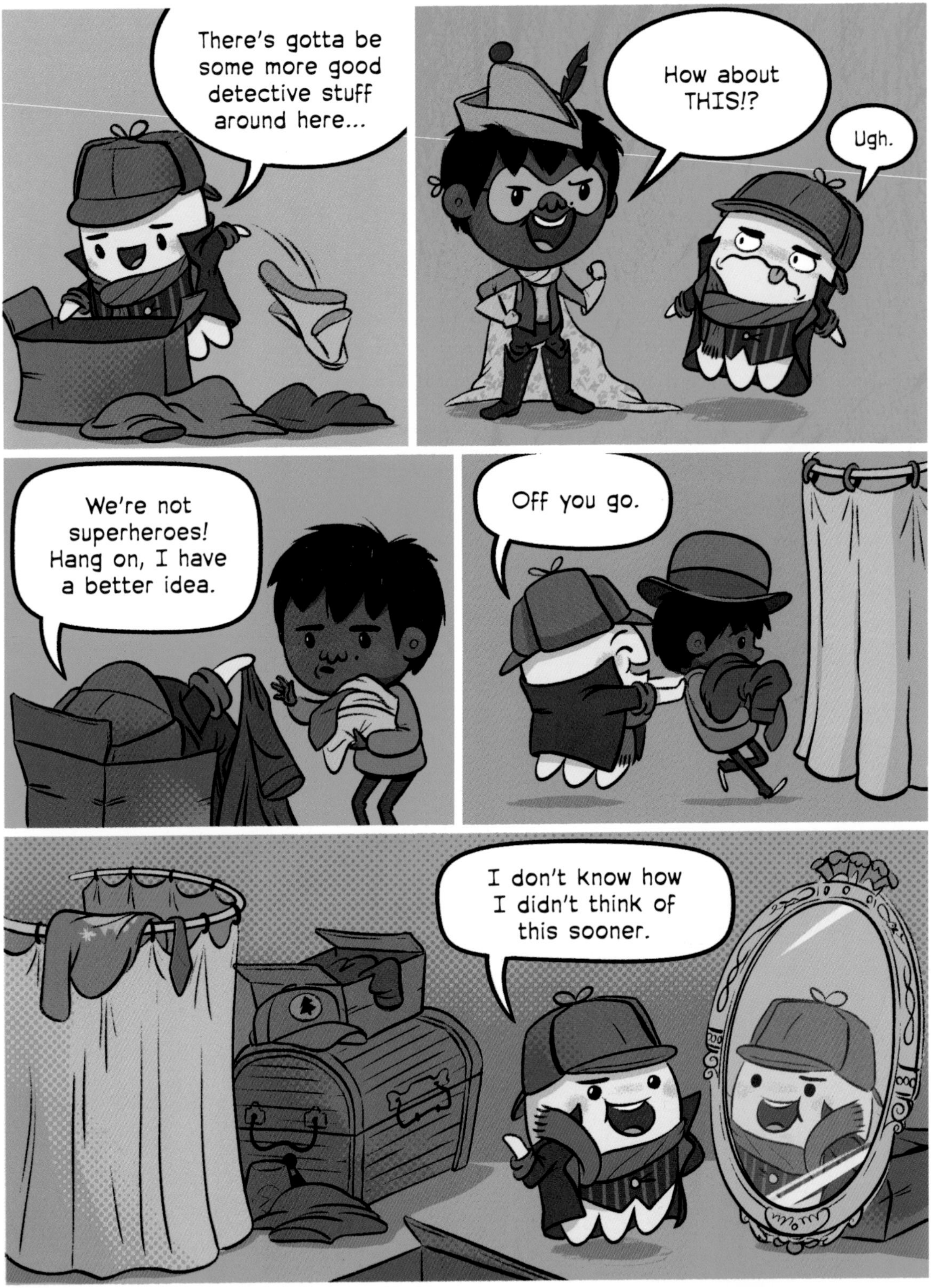
There's gotta be some more good detective stuff around here...
How about THIS!?
Ugh.
We're not superheroes! Hang on, I have a better idea.
Off you go.
I don't know how I didn't think of this sooner.

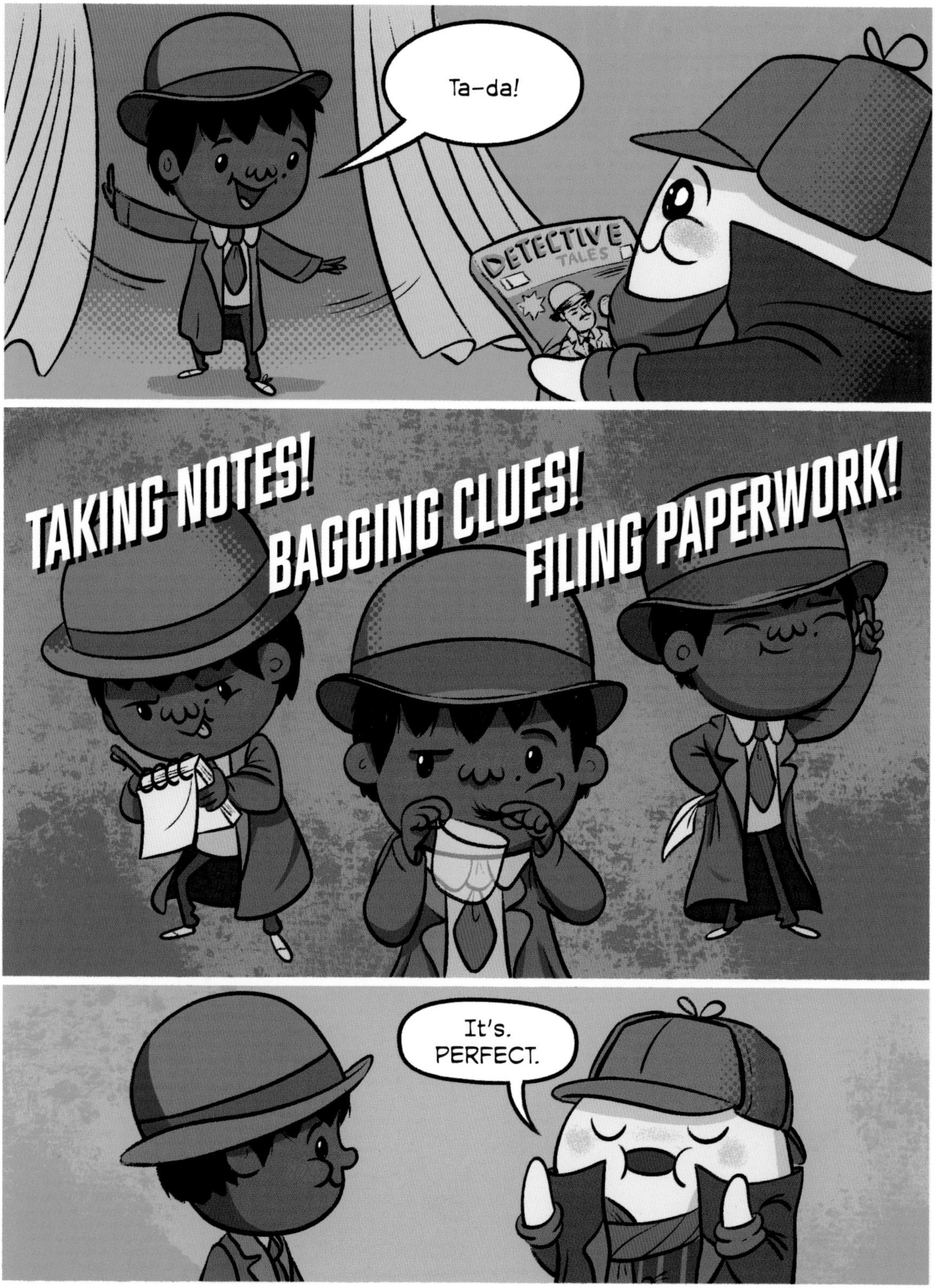

Ta-da!
DETECTIVE TALES
TAKING NOTES!
BAGGING CLUES!
FILING PAPERWORK!
It's. PERFECT.

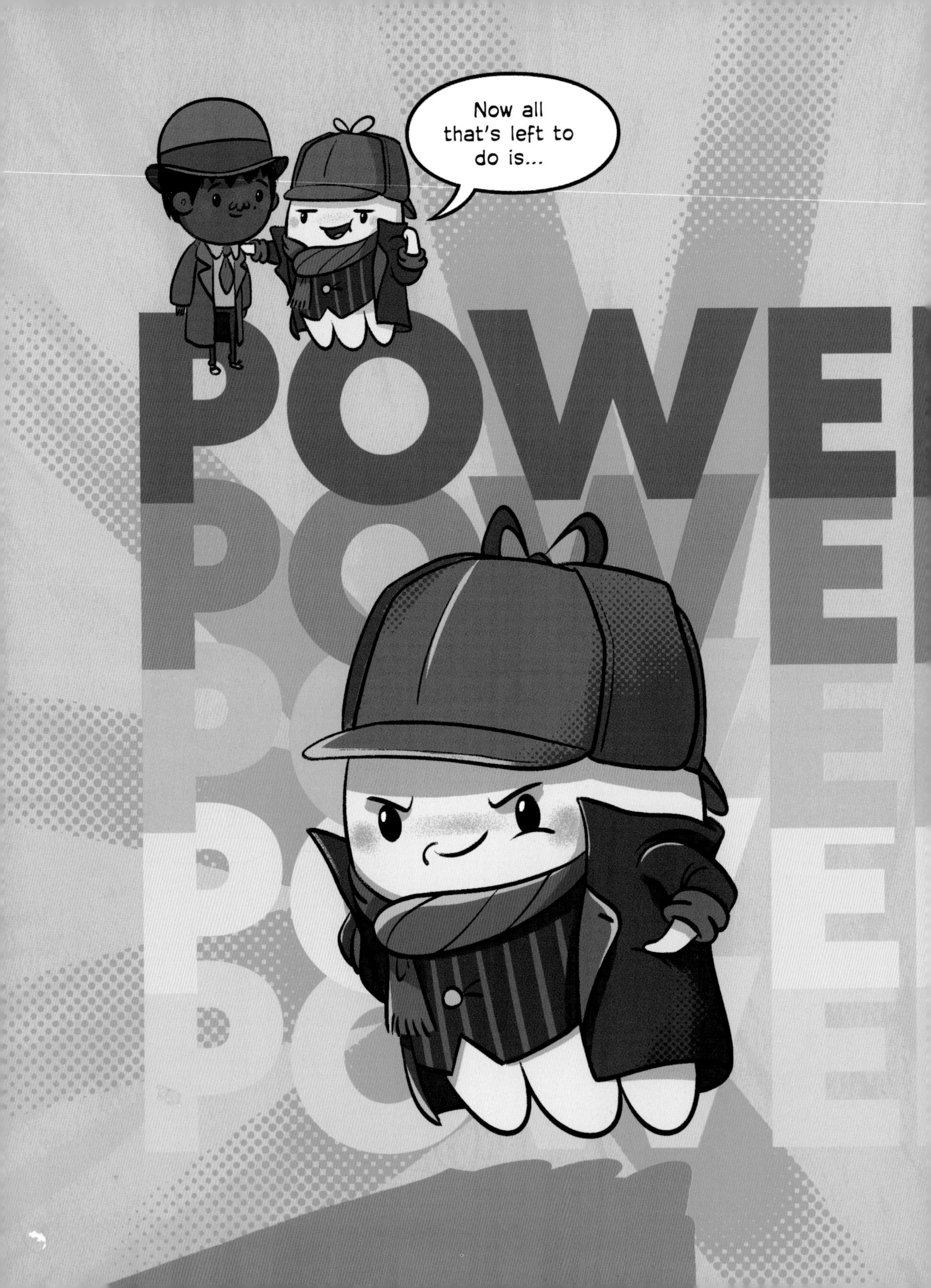
Now all that's left to do is...
POWE

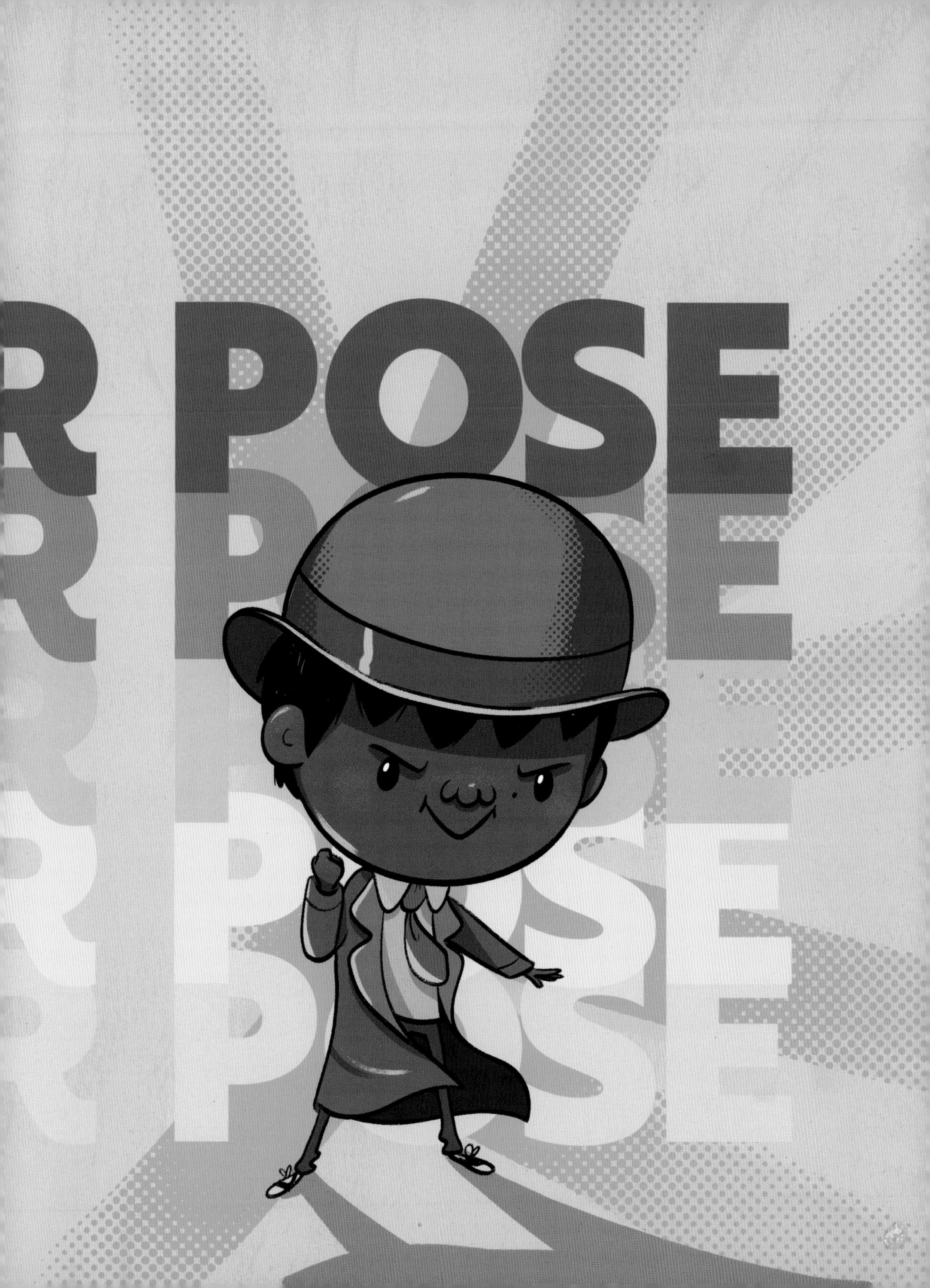
R POSE

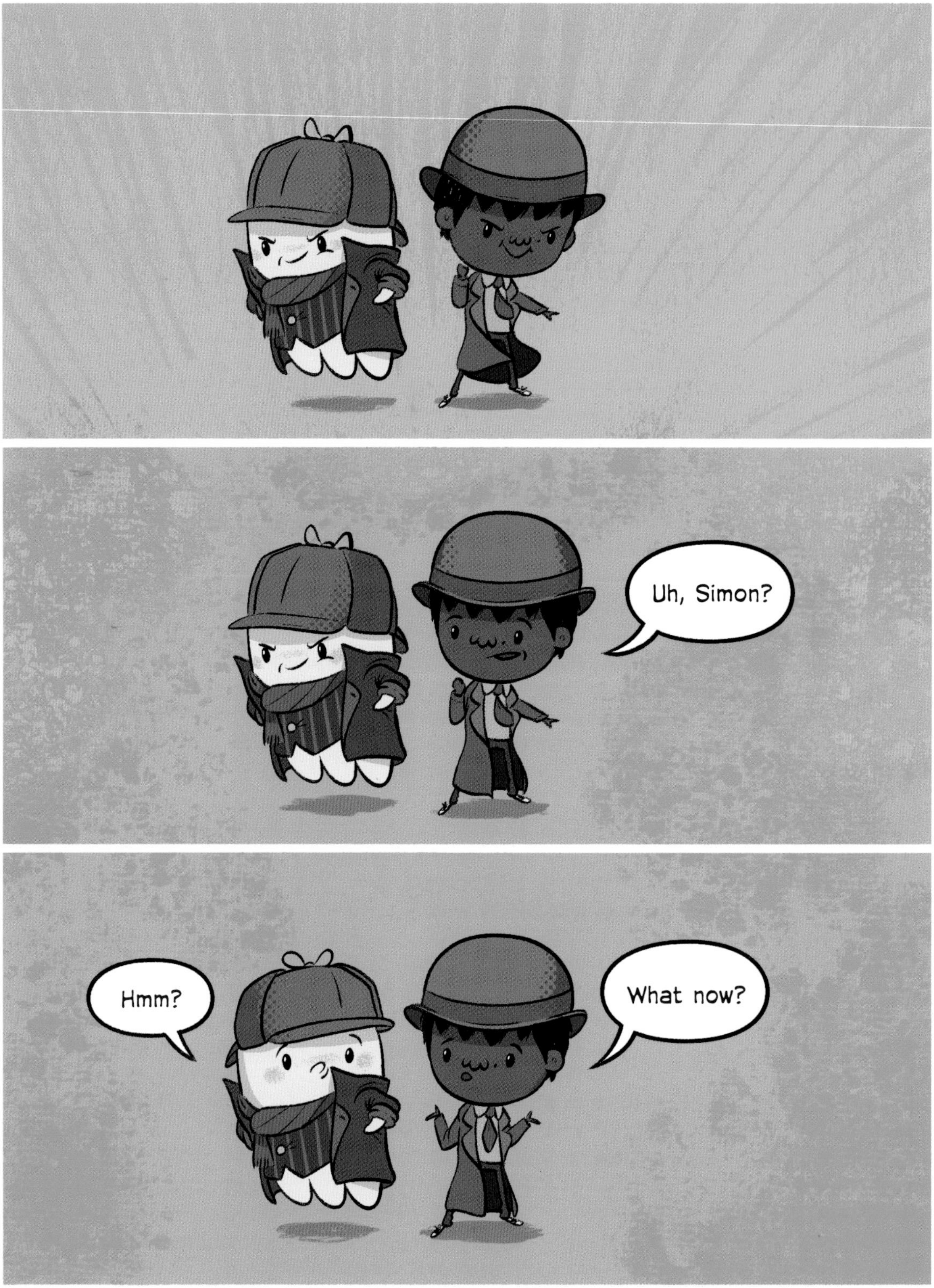
Uh, Simon?
Hmm?
What now?

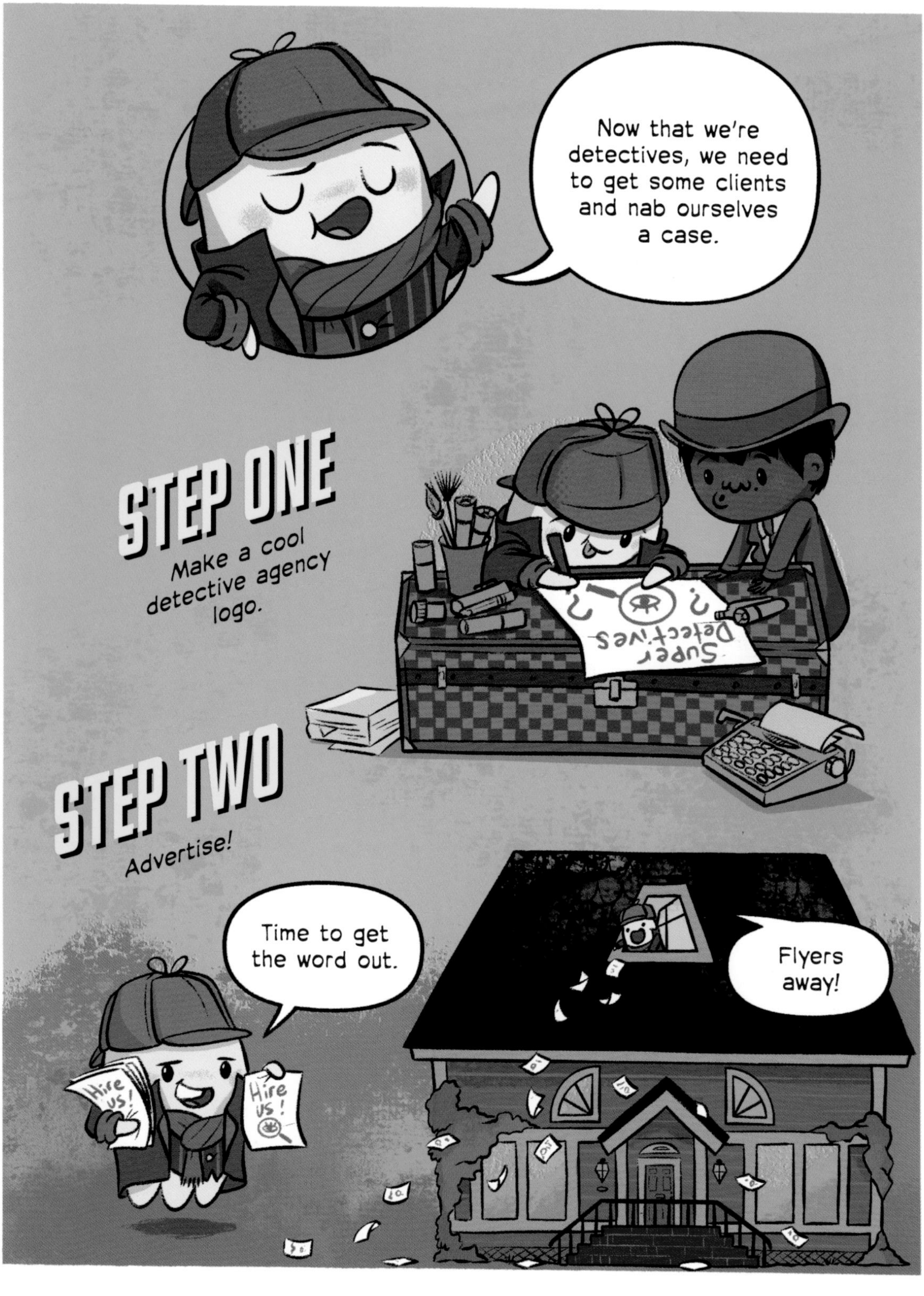
Now that we're detectives, we need to get some clients and nab ourselves a case.
STEP ONE
Make a cool detective agency logo.
Super Detectives
STEP TWO
Advertise!
Time to get the word out.
Hire us!
Hire us!
Flyers away!

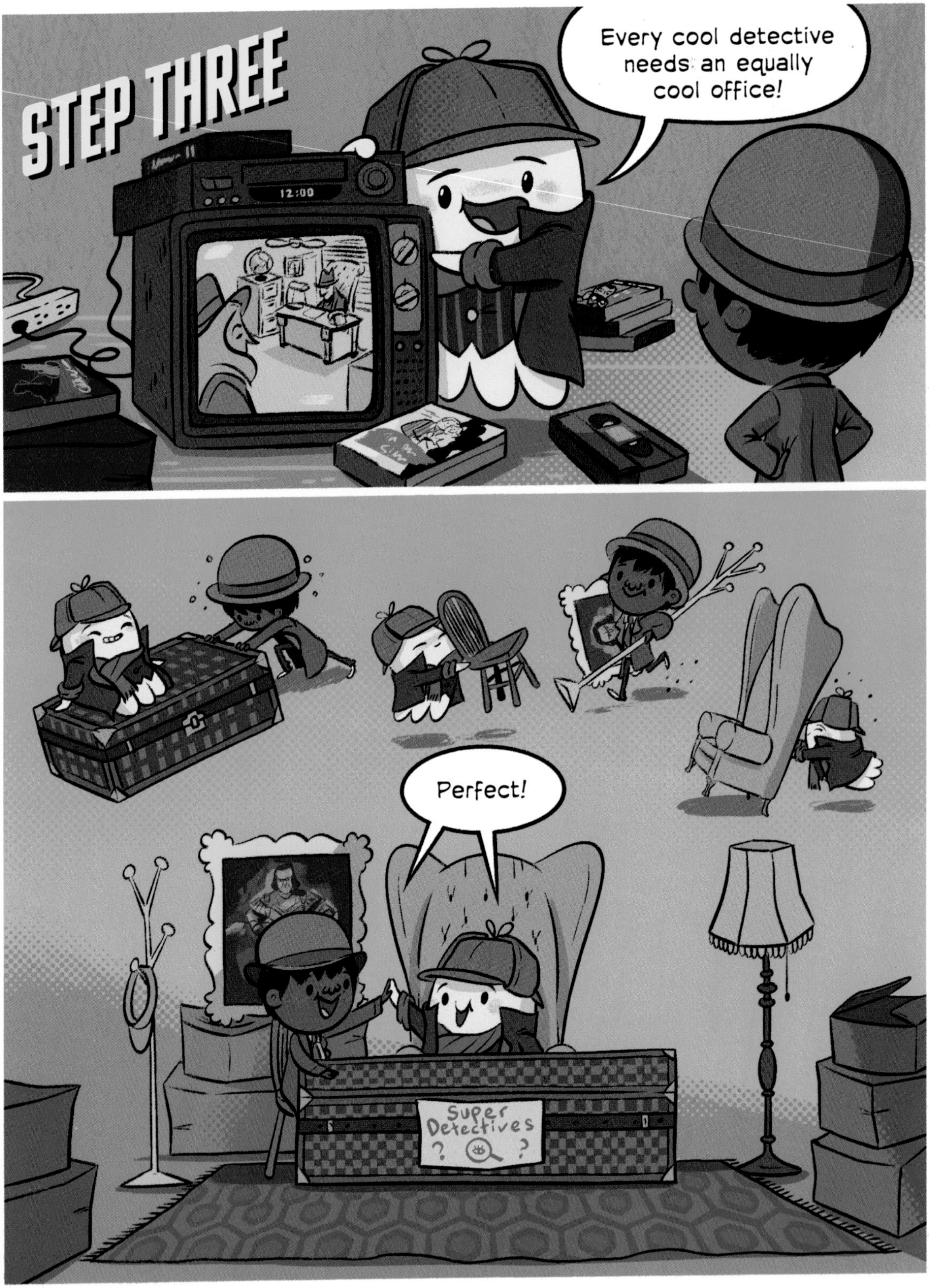
STEP THREE
Every cool detective needs an equally cool office!
Perfect!
Super Detectives
? ?

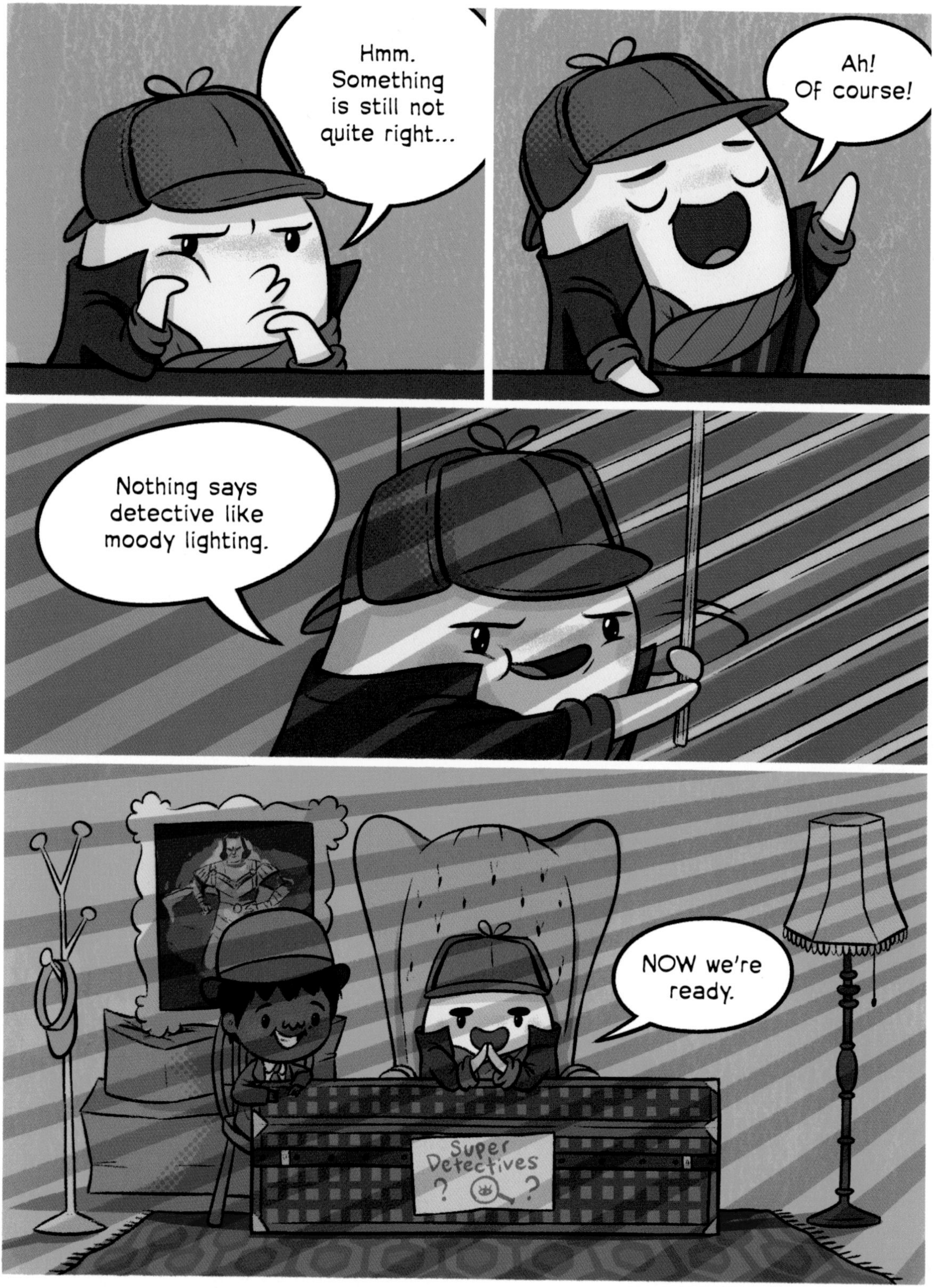
Hmm. Something is still not quite right...
Ah! Of course!
Nothing says detective like moody lighting.
NOW we're ready.
Super Detectives

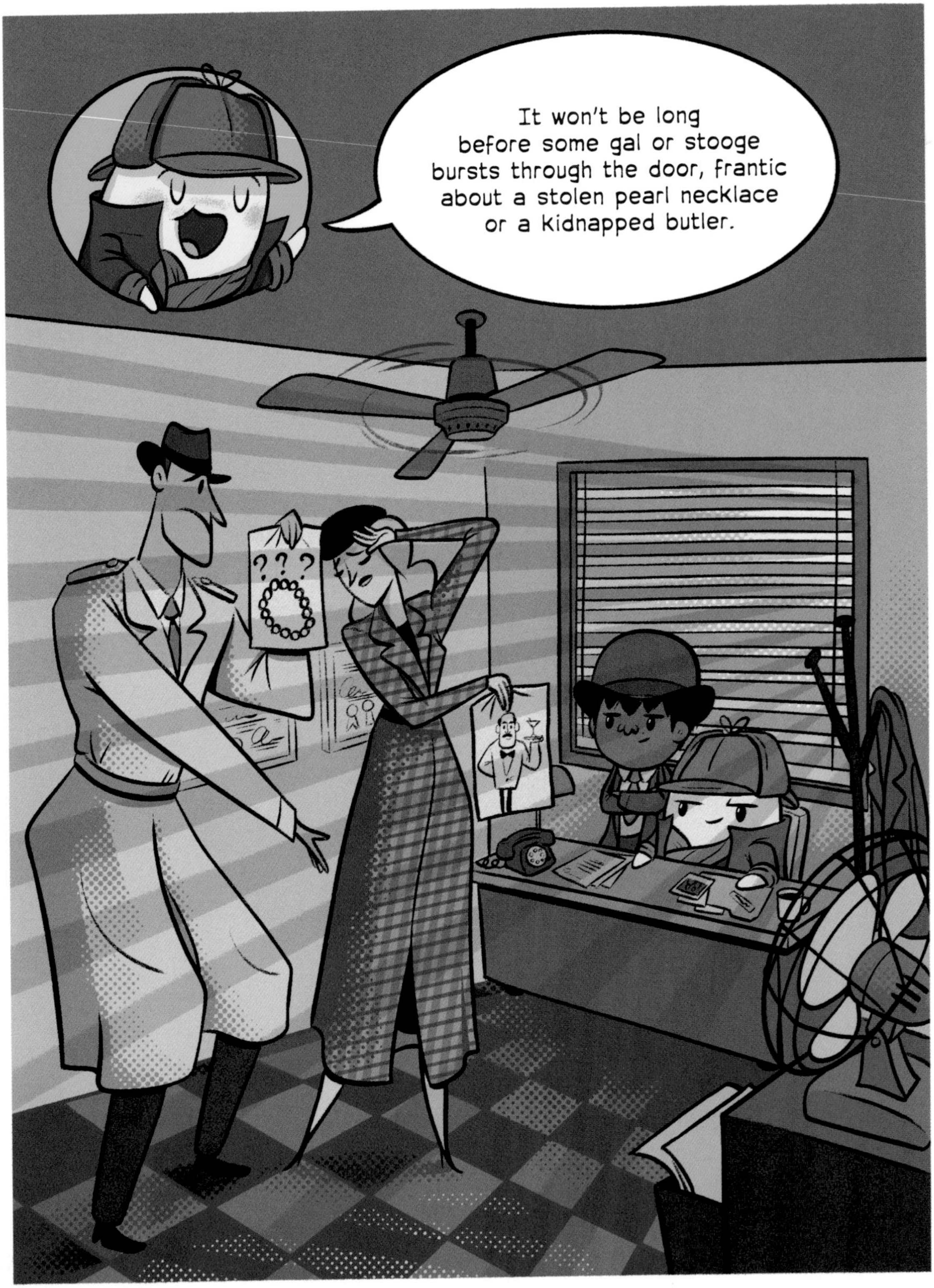
It won't be long before some gal or stooge bursts through the door, frantic about a stolen pearl necklace or a kidnapped butler.

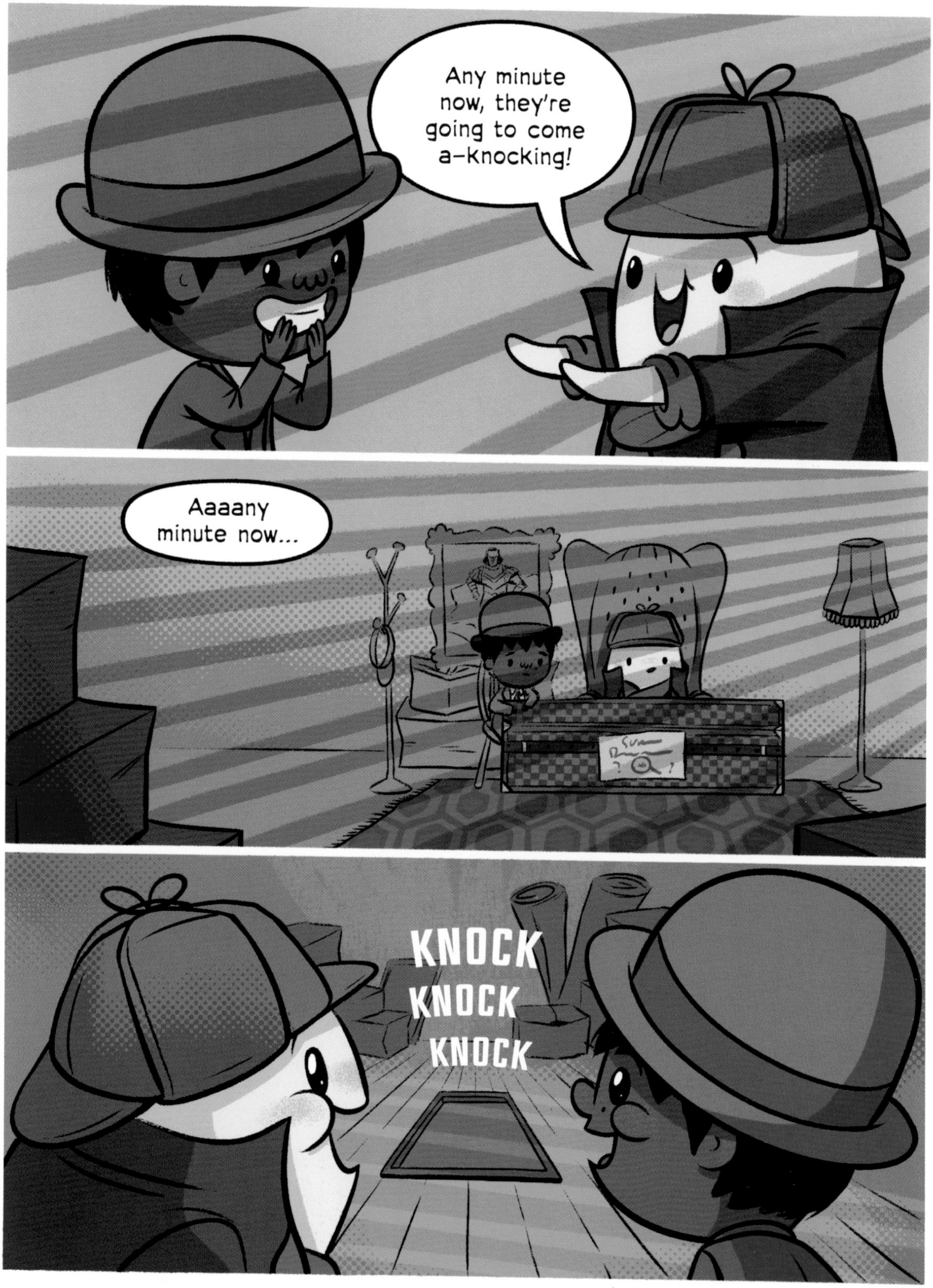

Any minute now, they're going to come a-knocking!
Aaaany minute now...
KNOCK
KNOCK
KNOCK

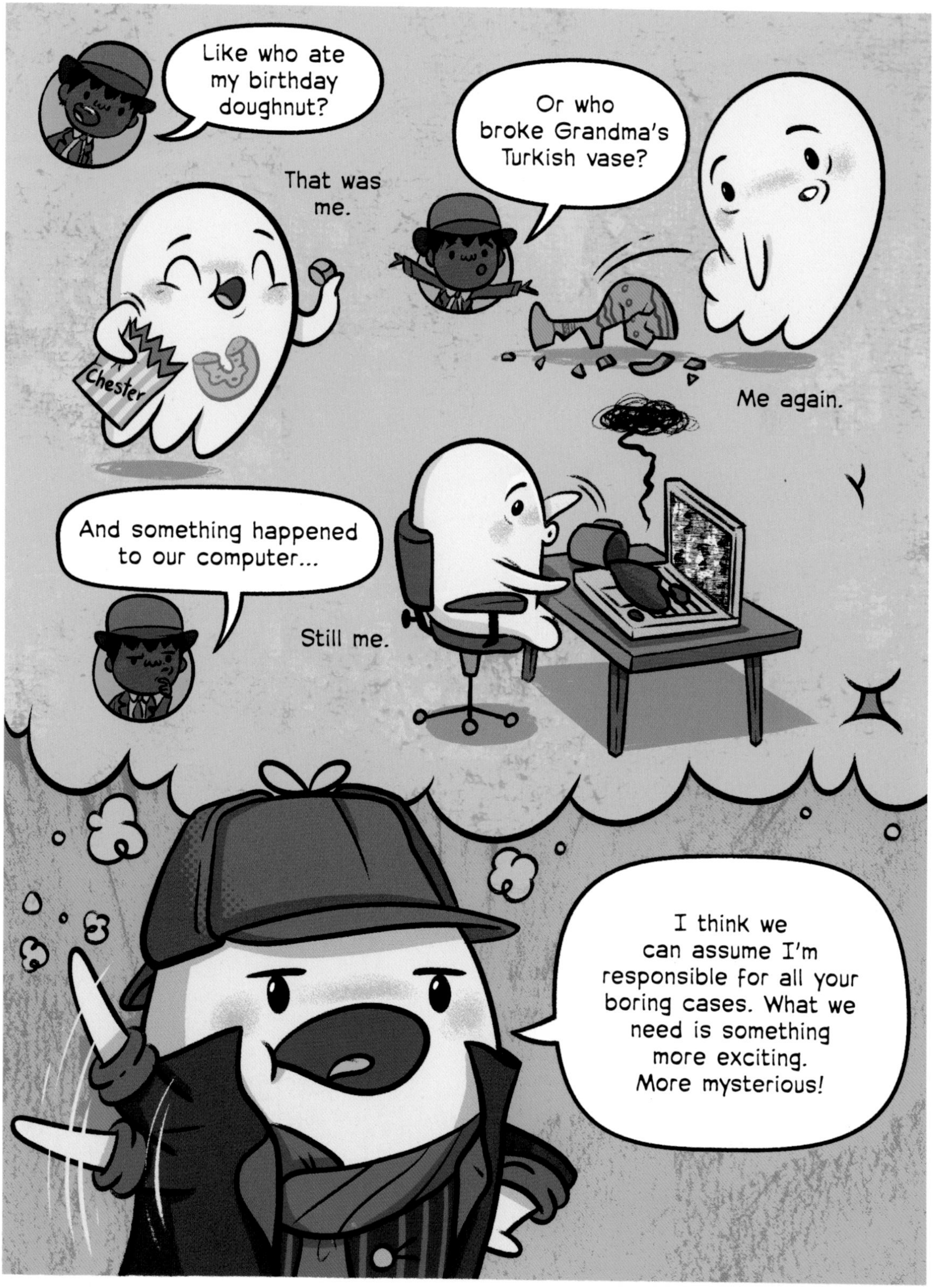
Like who ate my birthday doughnut?
That was me.
Chester
Or who broke Grandma's Turkish vase?
Me again.
And something happened to our computer...
Still me.
I think we can assume I'm responsible for all your boring cases. What we need is something more exciting. More mysterious!

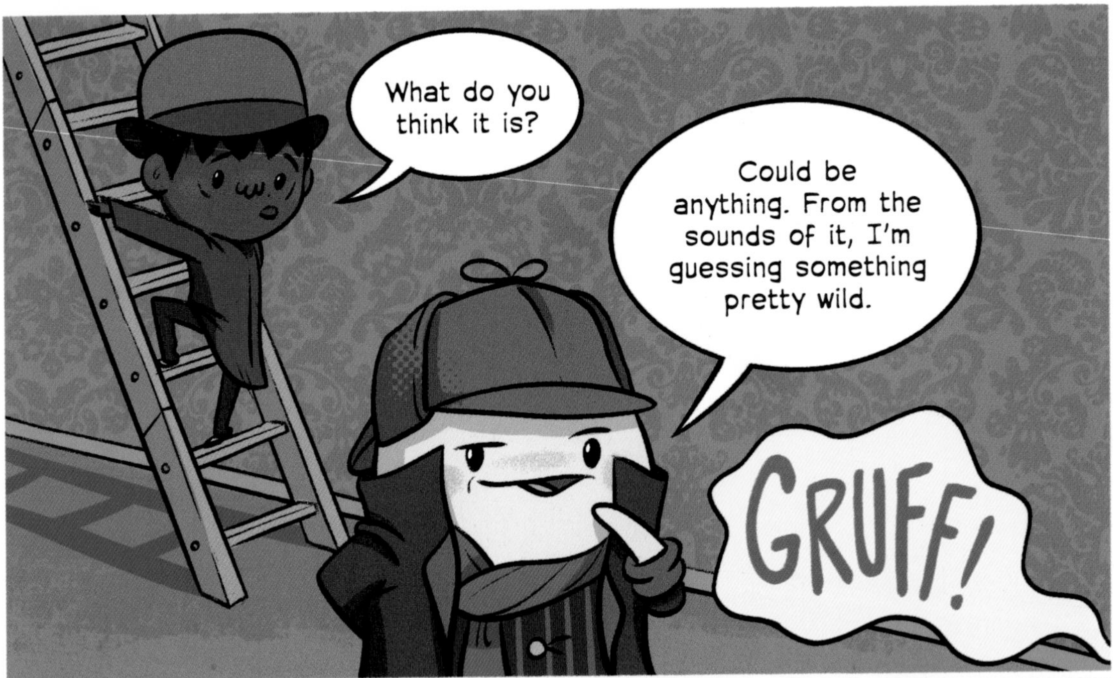
What do you think it is?
Could be anything. From the sounds of it, I'm guessing something pretty wild.
GRUFF!

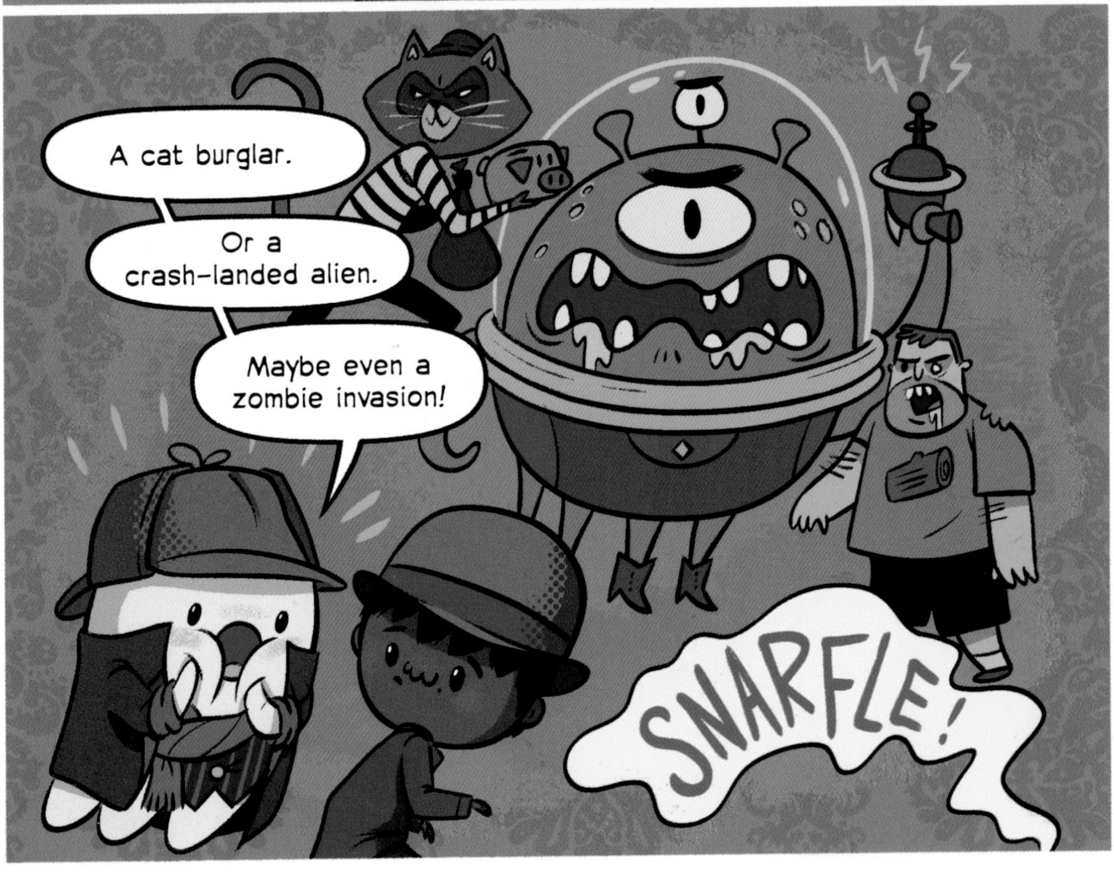
A cat burglar.
Or a crash-landed alien.
Maybe even a zombie invasion!
SNARFLE!

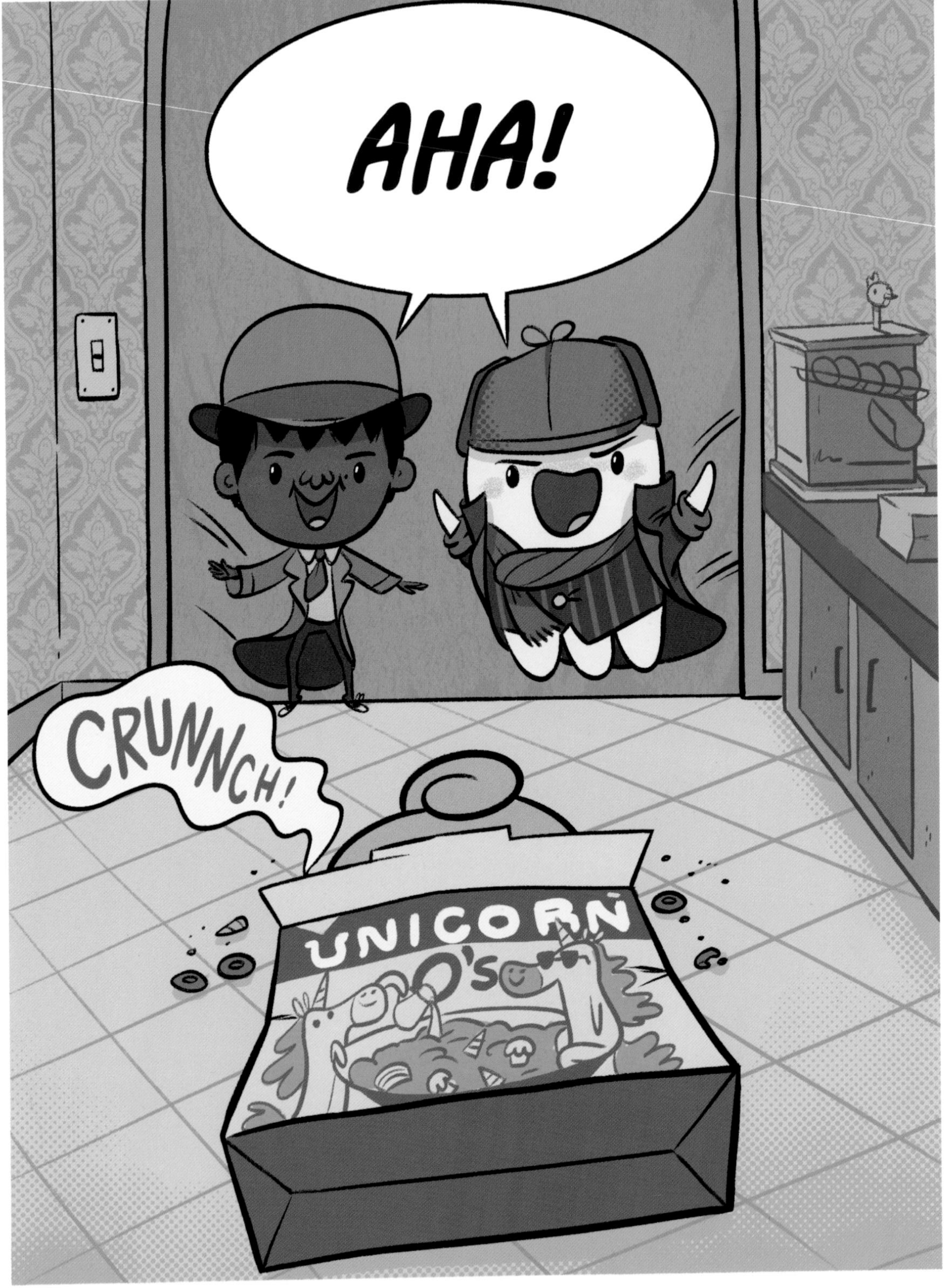
AHA!
CRUNNCH!
UNICORN
O's

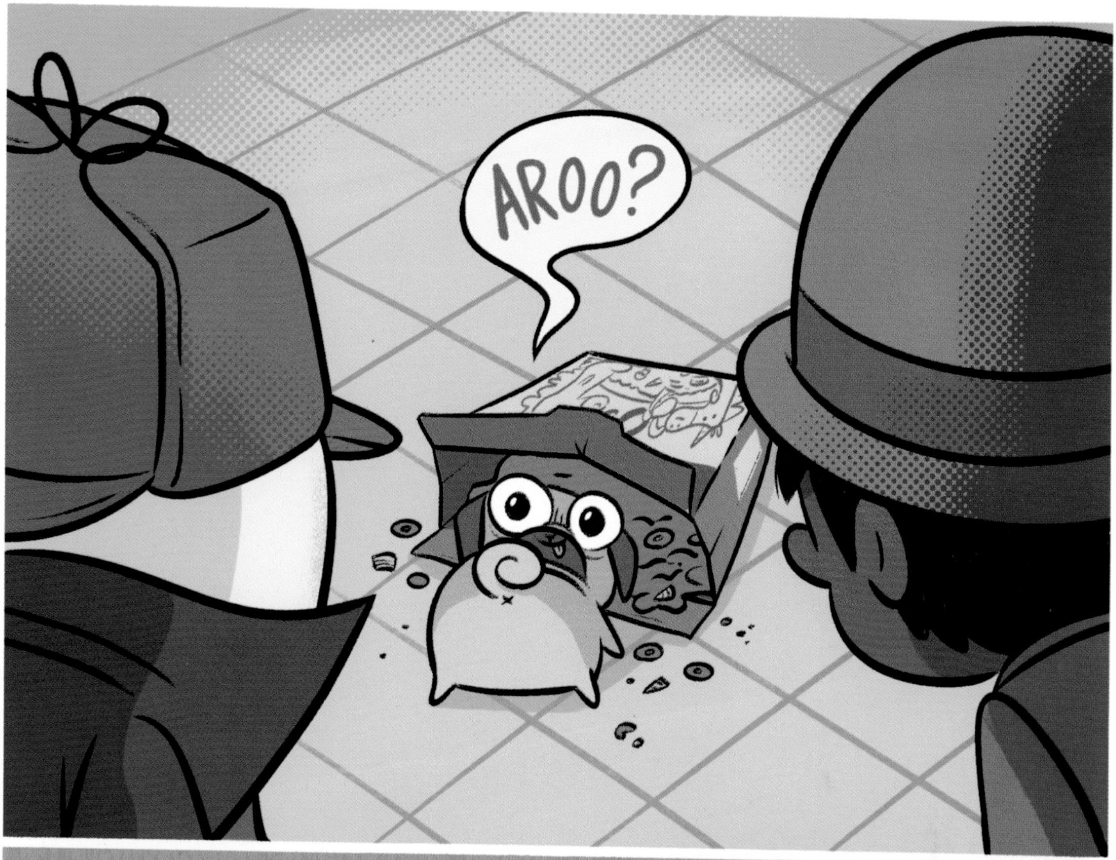
AROO?

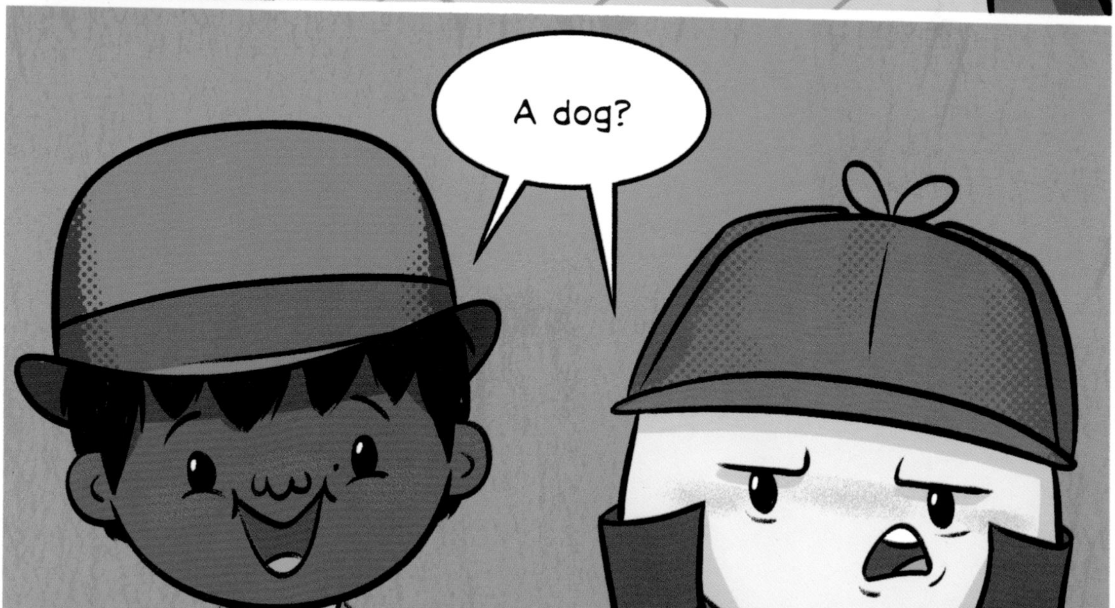
A dog?

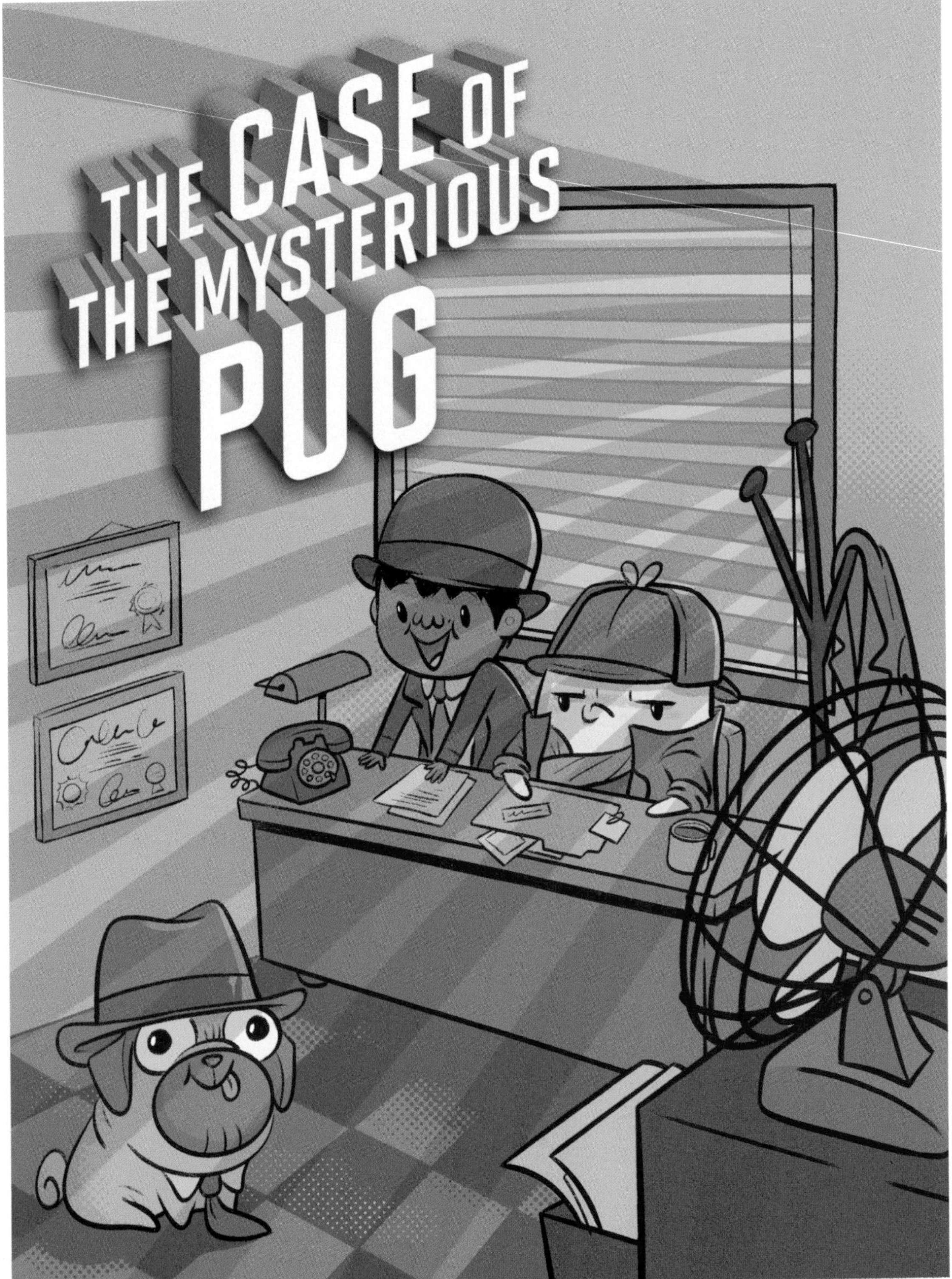
THE CASE OF
THE MYSTERIOUS
PUG

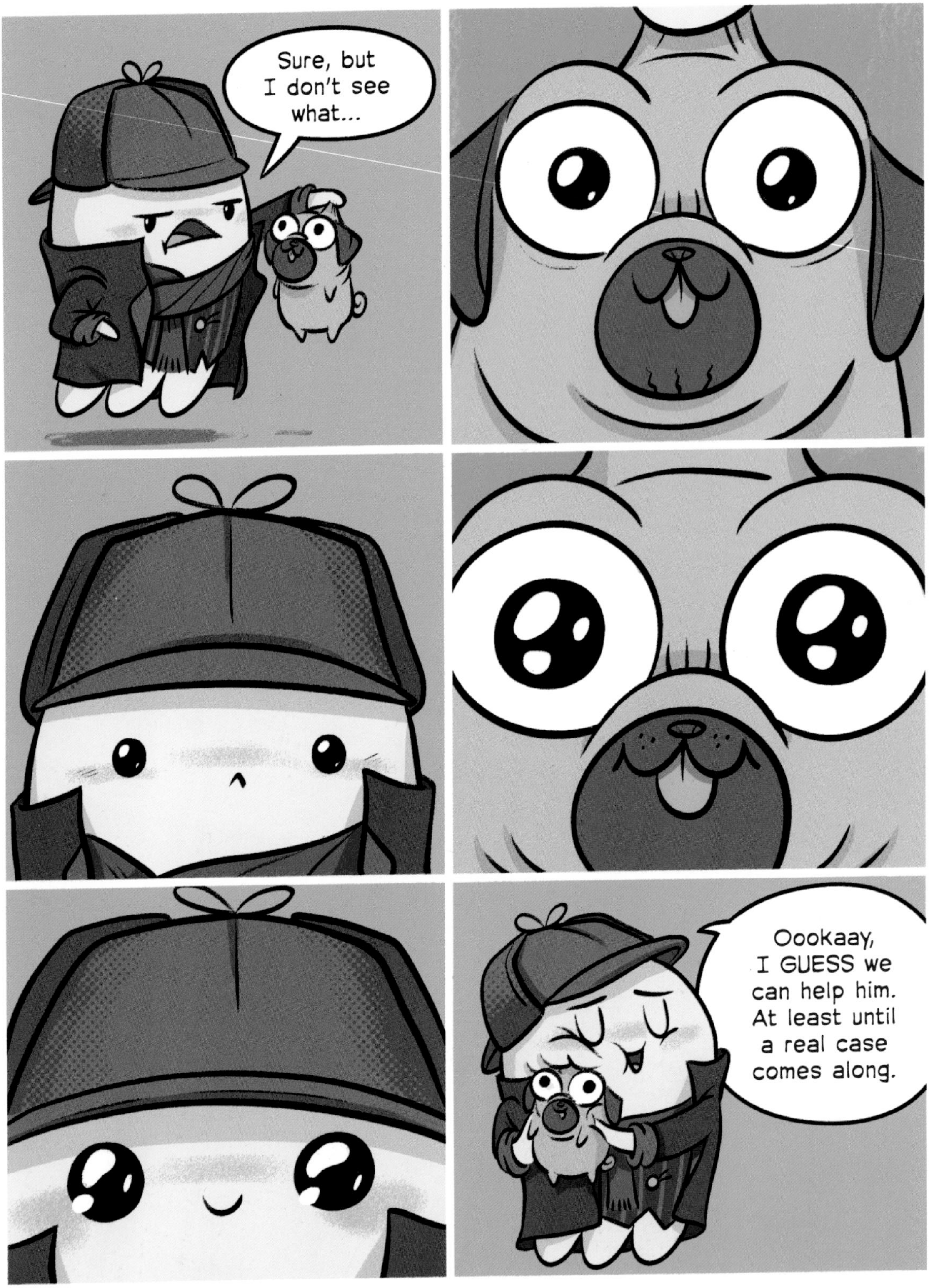

Sure, but I don't see what...
Oookaay, I GUESS we can help him. At least until a real case comes along.

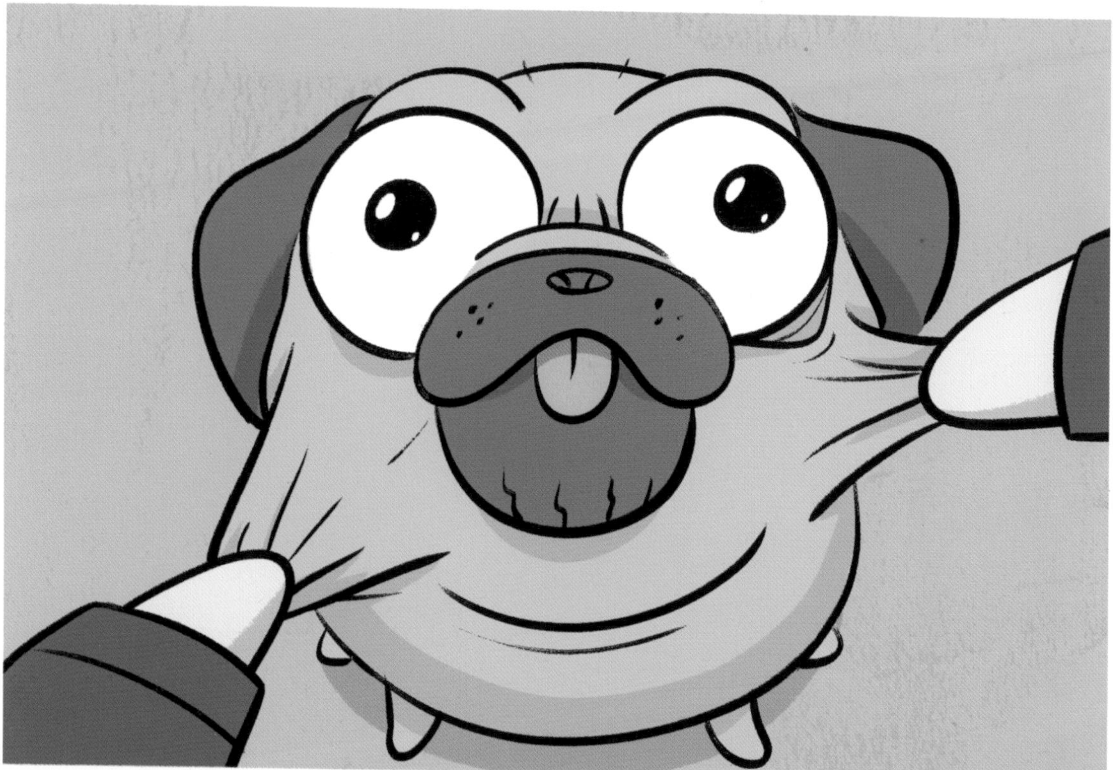

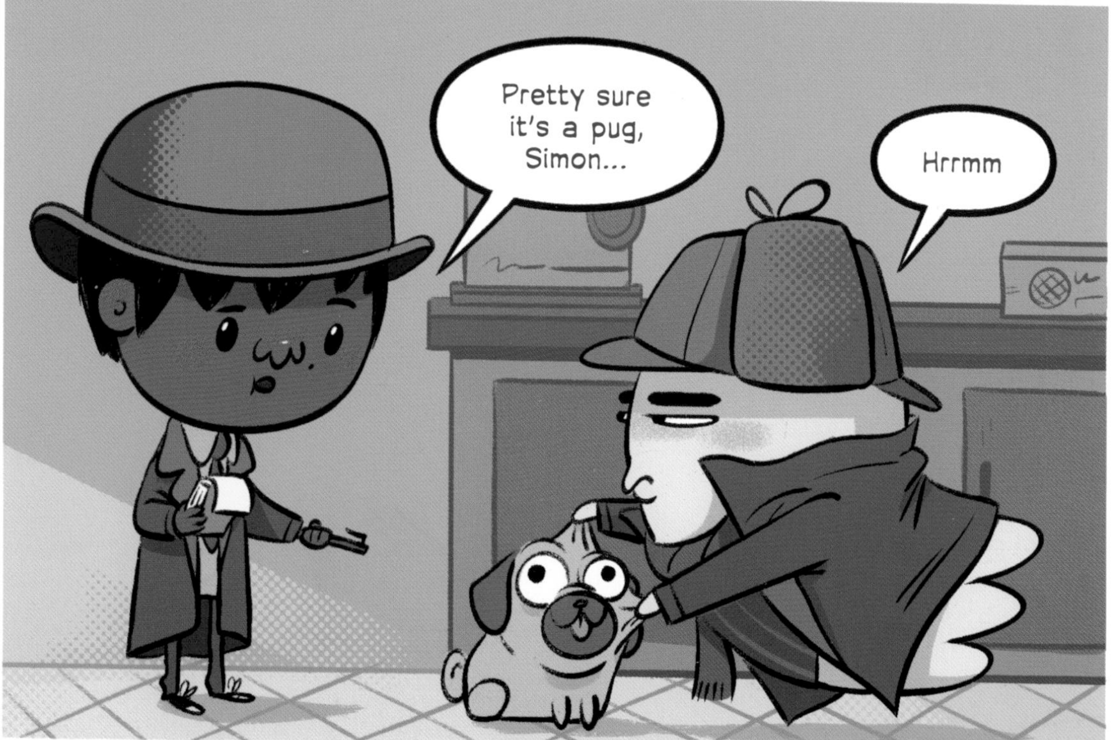
Pretty sure it's a pug, Simon...
Hrrmm

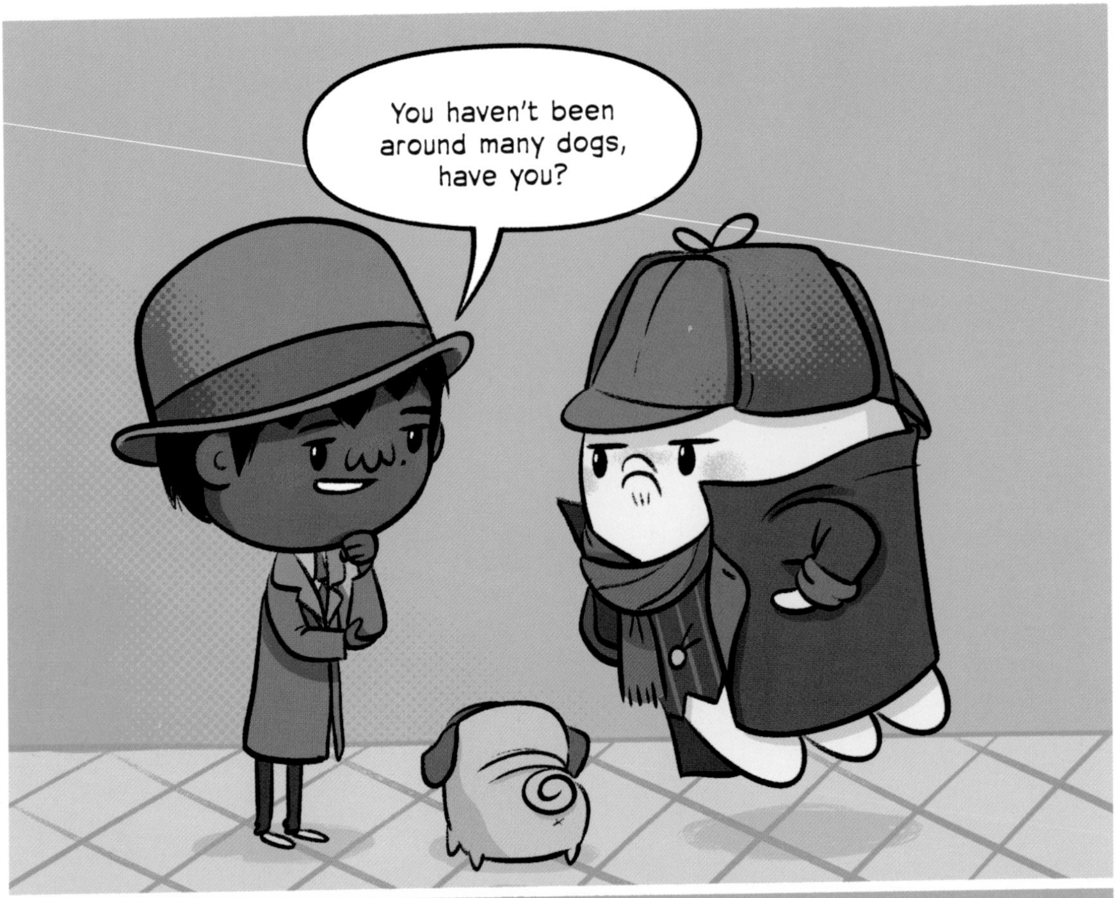
You haven't been around many dogs, have you?

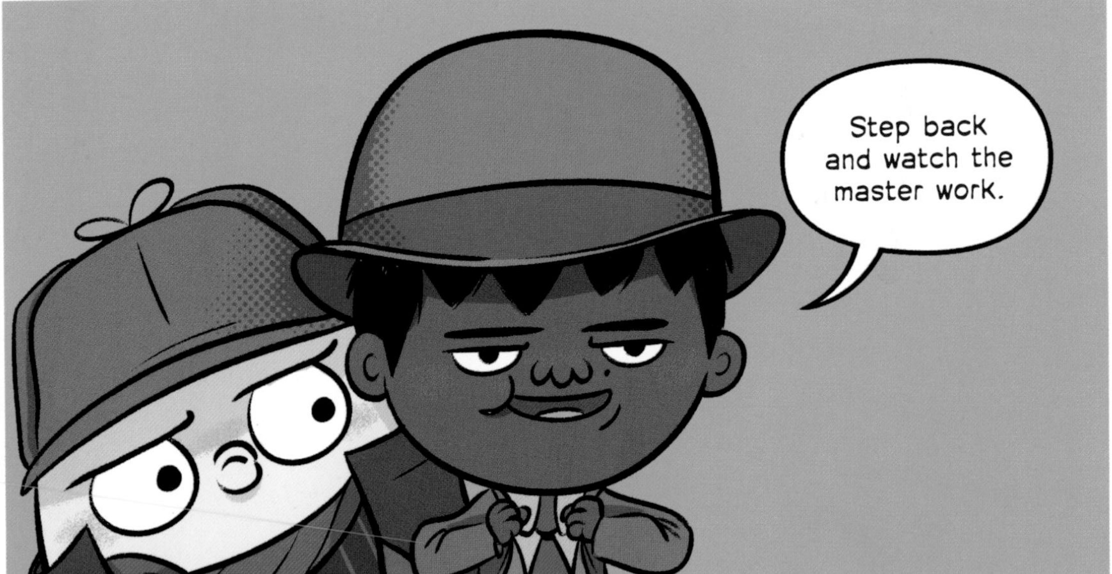
Step back and watch the master work.

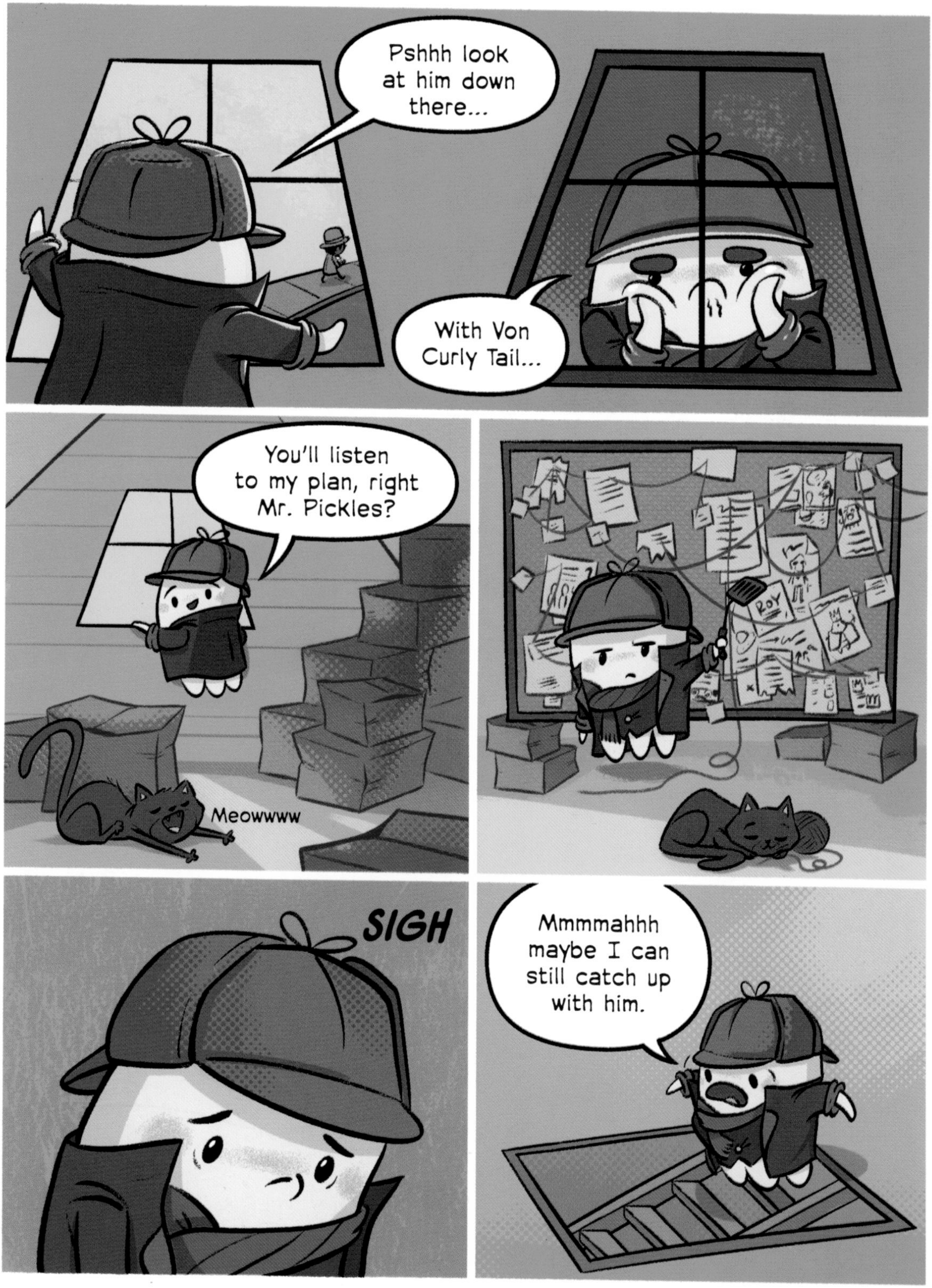
Pshhh look at him down there...
With Von Curly Tail...
You'll listen to my plan, right Mr. Pickles?
Meowwww
ROY
SIGH
Mmmmahhh maybe I can still catch up with him.

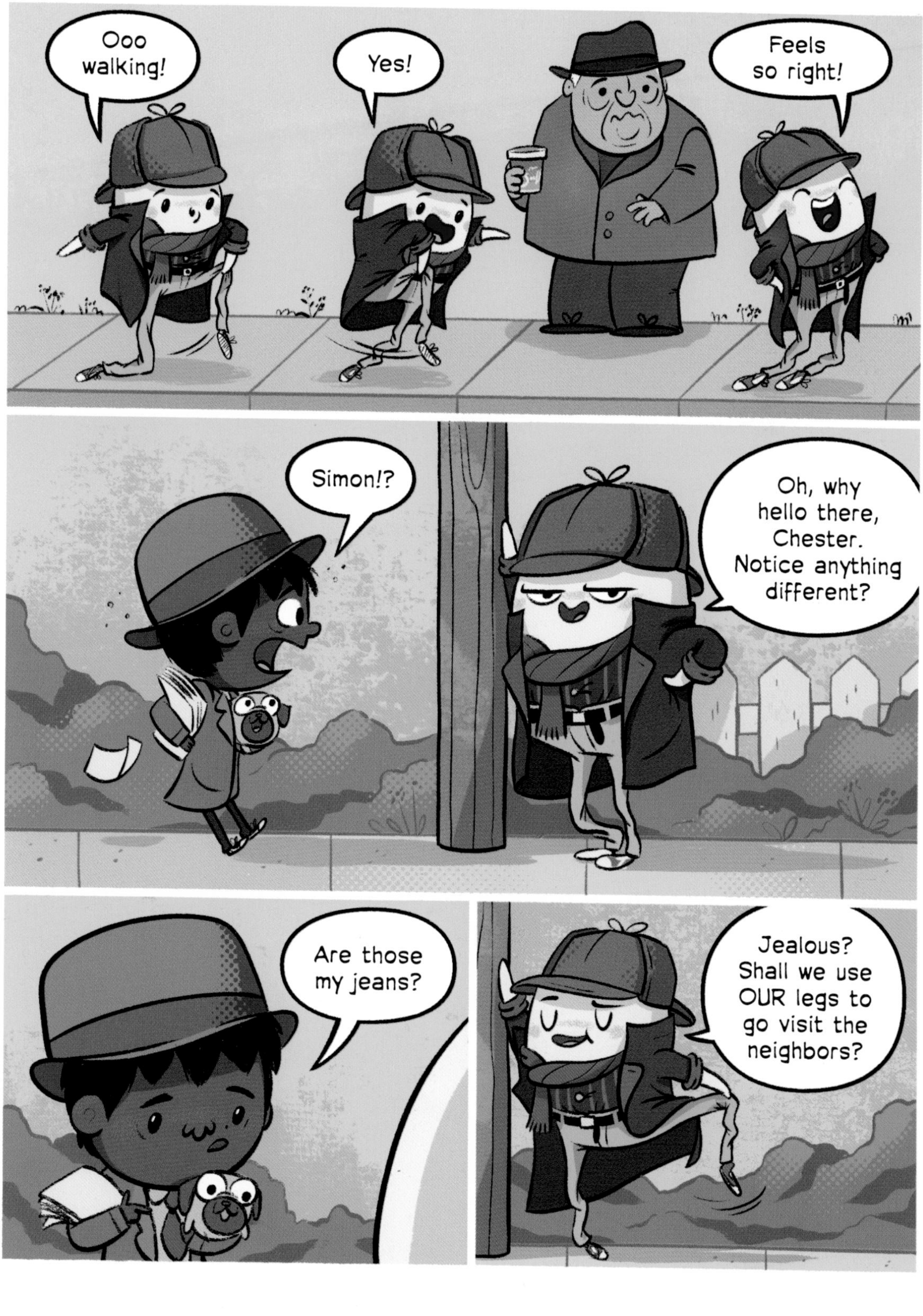
Ooo walking!
Yes!
Feels so right!
Simon!?
Oh, why hello there, Chester. Notice anything different?
Are those my jeans?
Jealous? Shall we use OUR legs to go visit the neighbors?

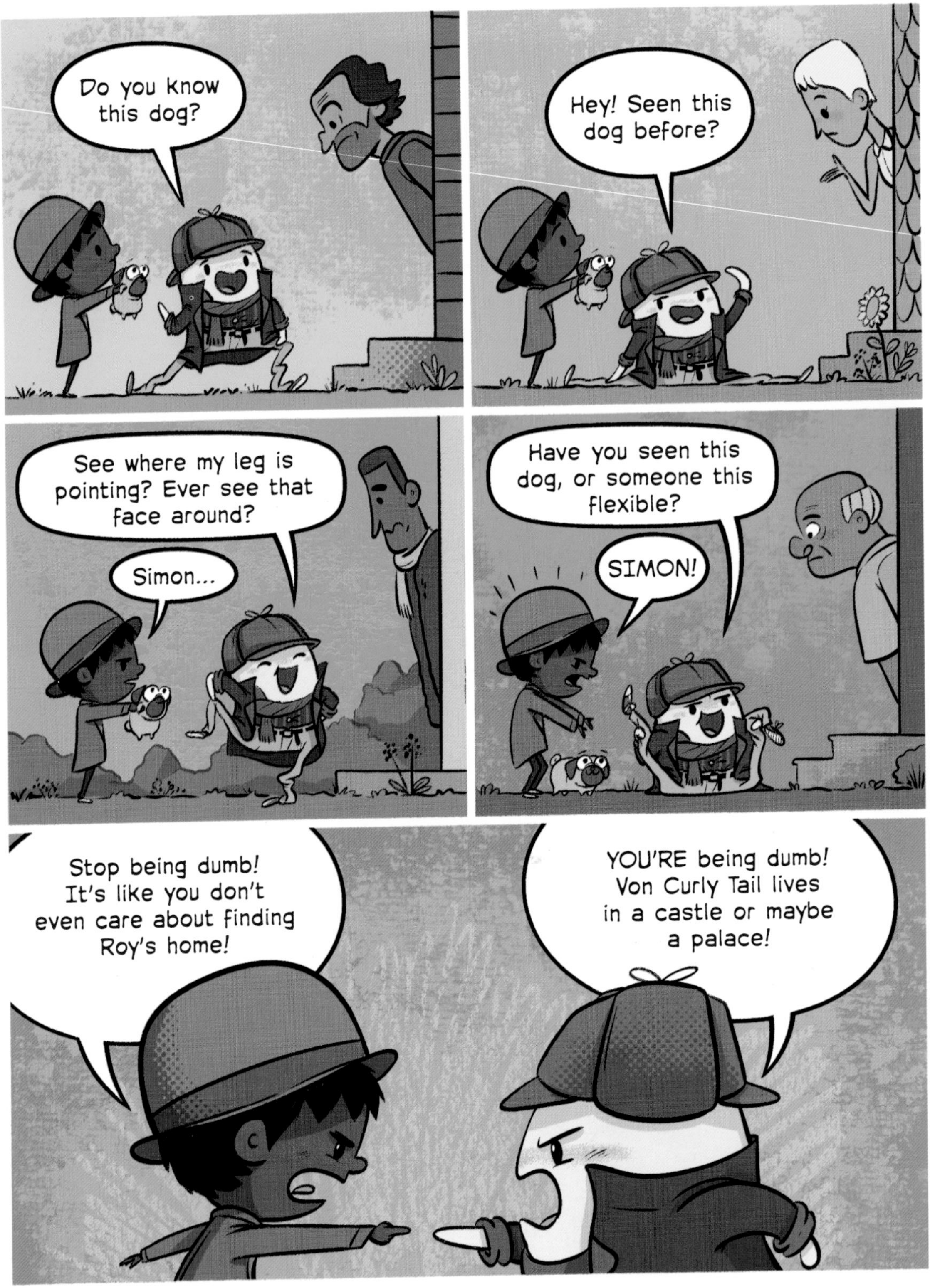
Do you know this dog?
Hey! Seen this dog before?
See where my leg is pointing? Ever see that face around?
Simon...
Have you seen this dog, or someone this flexible?
SIMON!
Stop being dumb! It's like you don't even care about finding Roy's home!
YOU'RE being dumb! Von Curly Tail lives in a castle or maybe a palace!

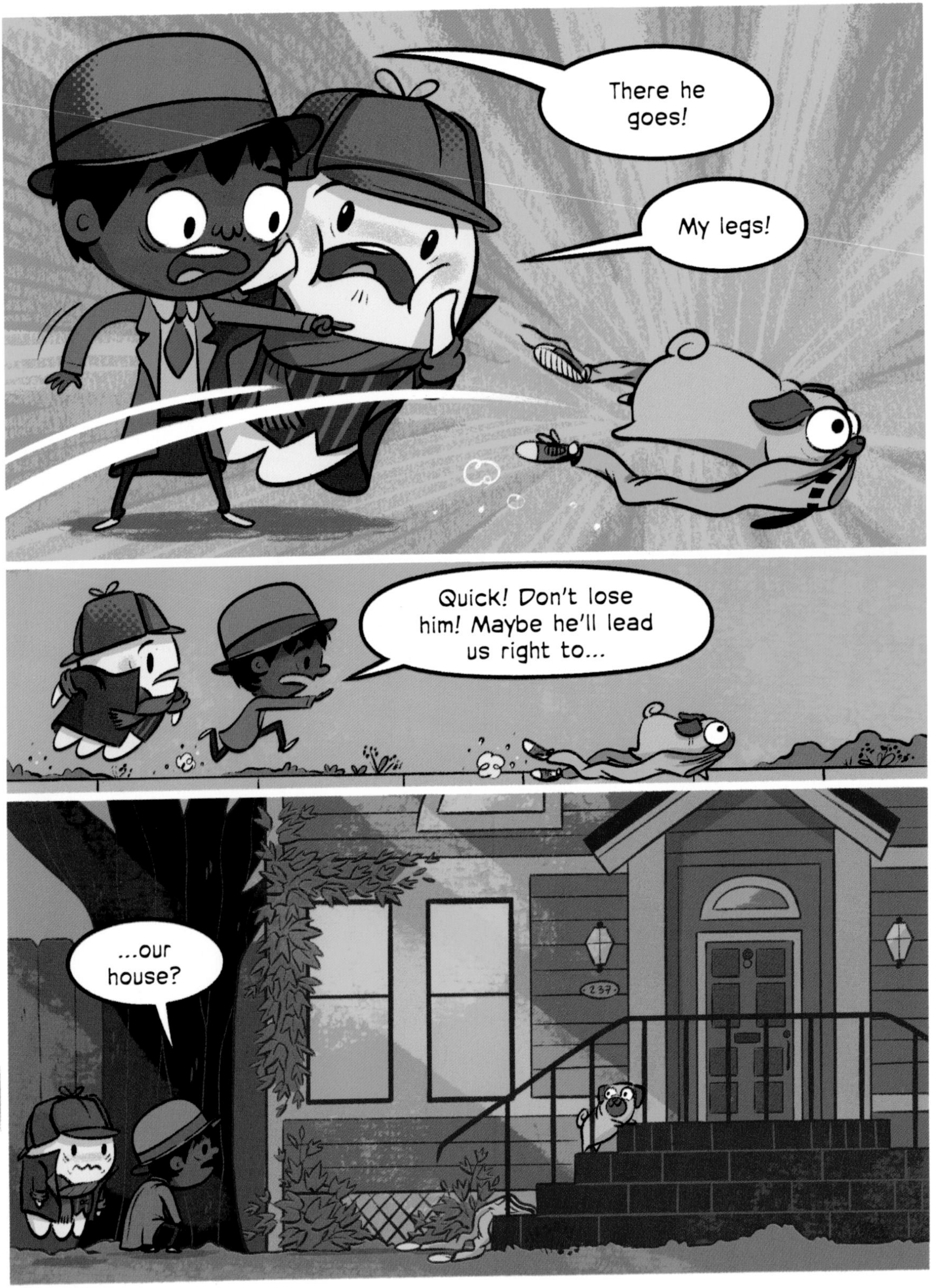
There he goes!
My legs!
Quick! Don't lose him! Maybe he'll lead us right to...
...our house?
237

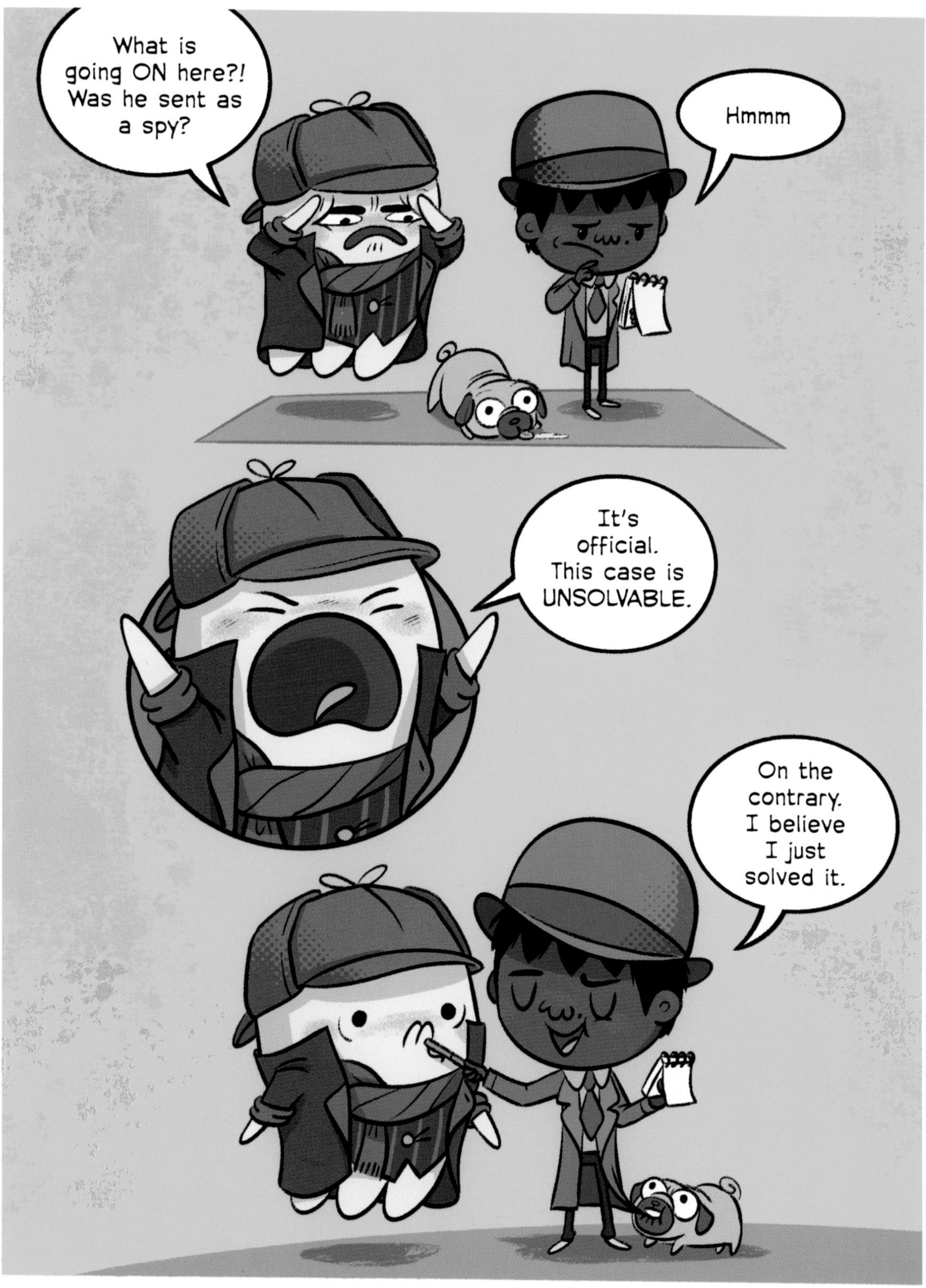
What is going ON here?! Was he sent as a spy?
Hmmm
It's official. This case is UNSOLVABLE.
On the contrary. I believe I just solved it.

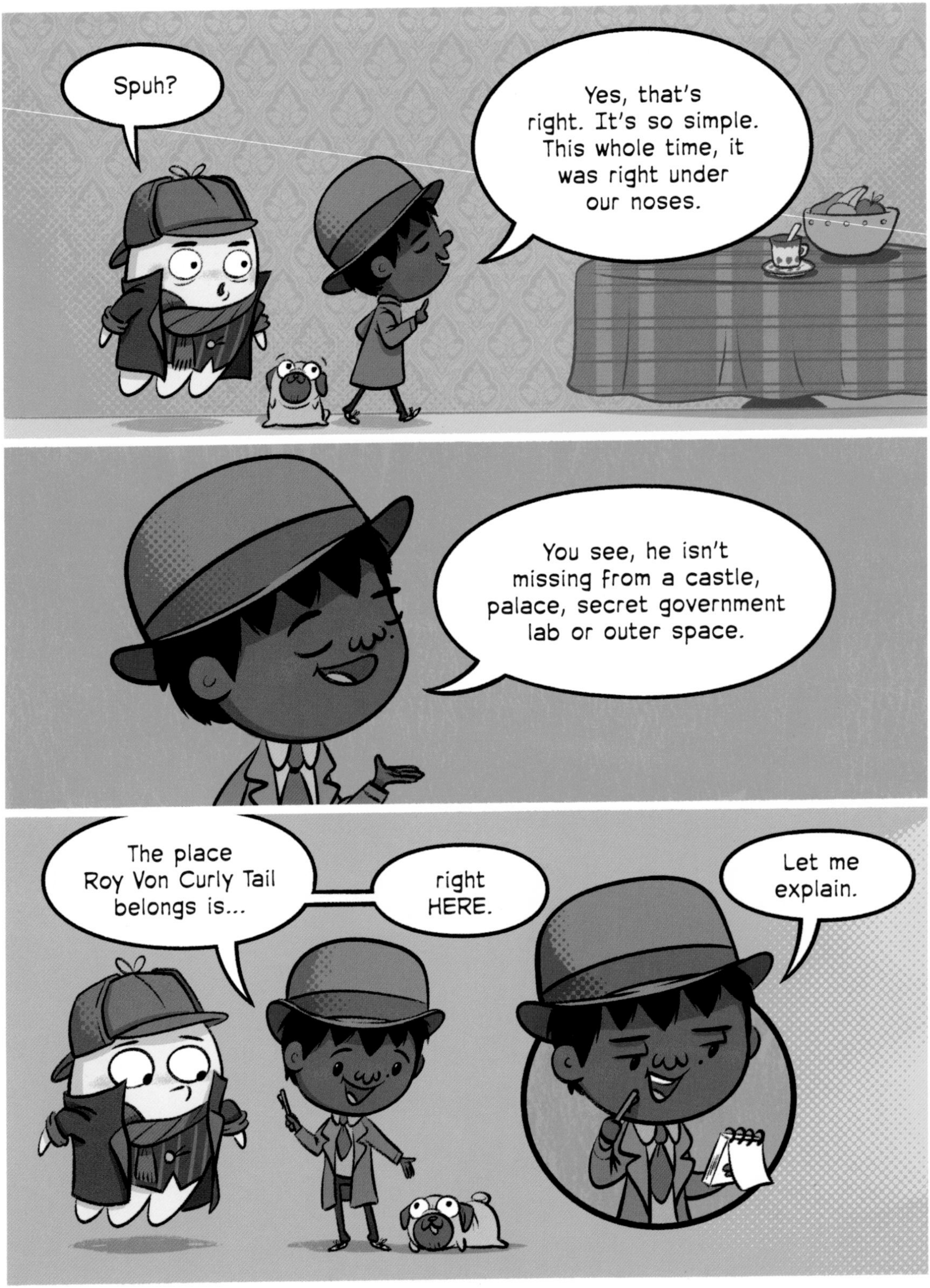
Spuh?
Yes, that's right. It's so simple. This whole time, it was right under our noses.
You see, he isn't missing from a castle, palace, secret government lab or outer space.
The place Roy Von Curly Tail belongs is...
right HERE.
Let me explain.

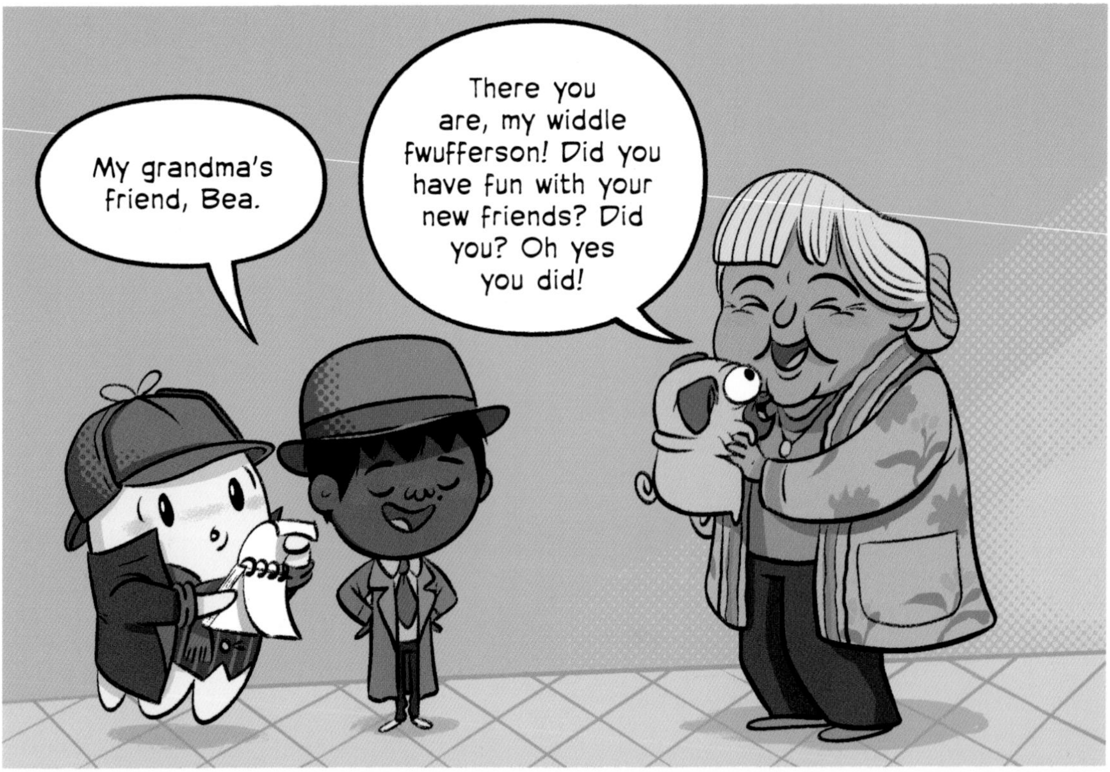
My grandma's friend, Bea.
There you are, my widdle fwufferson! Did you have fun with your new friends? Did you? Oh yes you did!

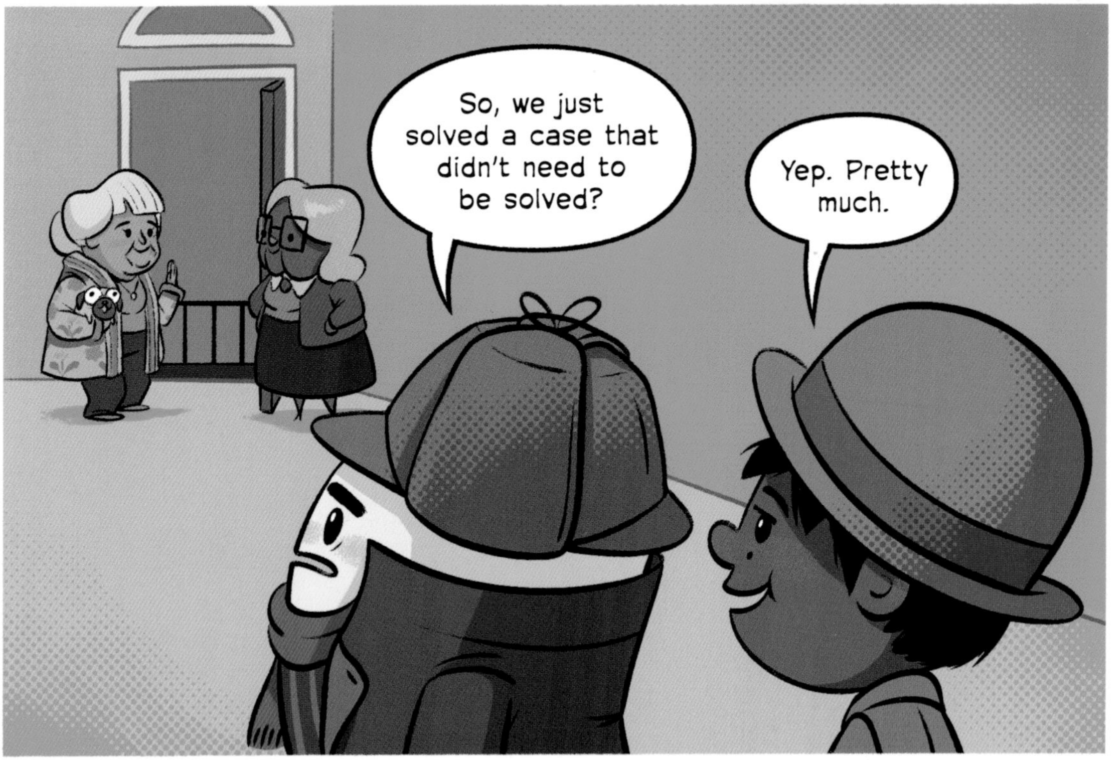
So, we just solved a case that didn't need to be solved?
Yep. Pretty much.

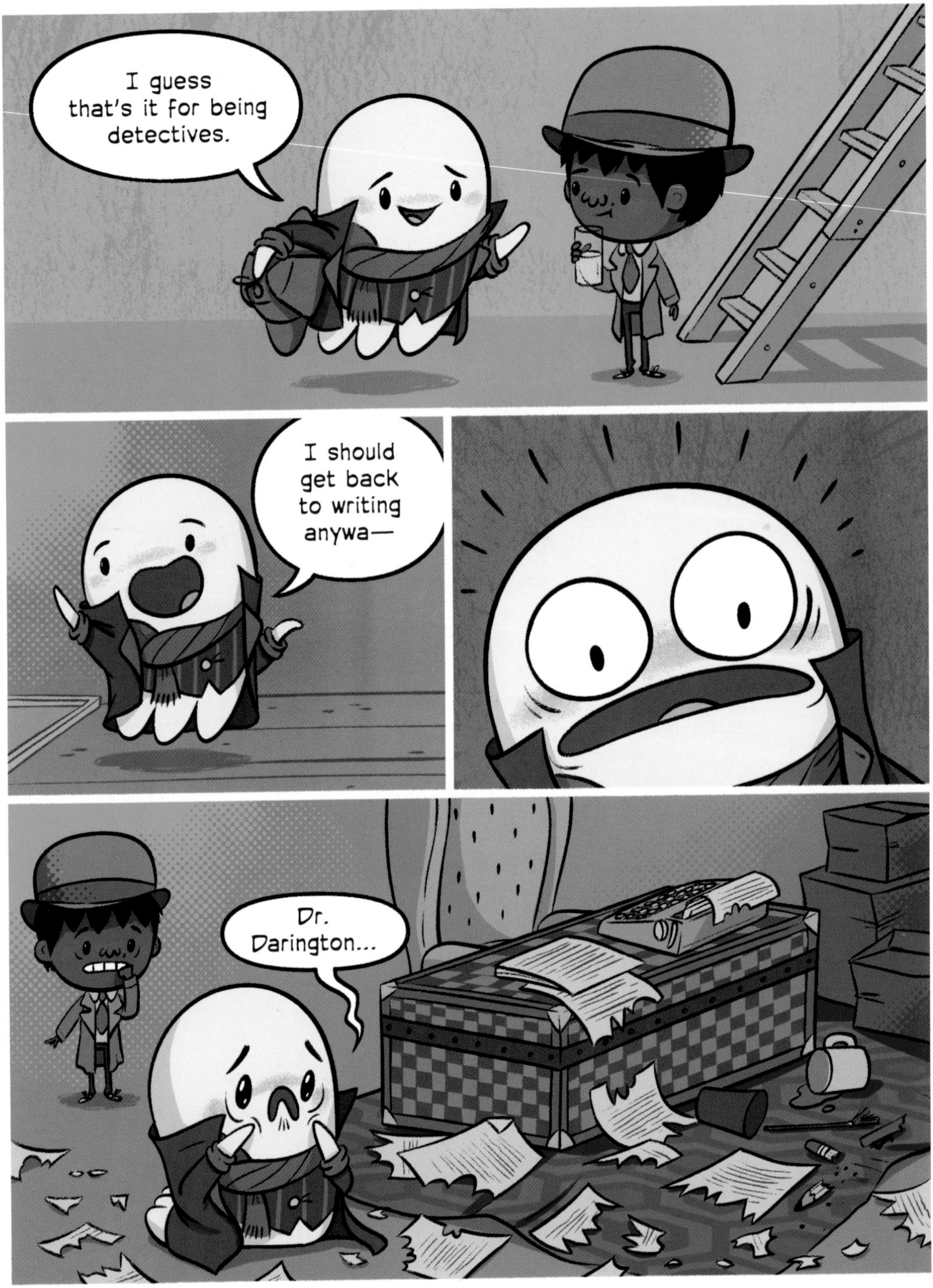
I guess that's it for being detectives.
I should get back to writing anywa—
Dr. Darington...

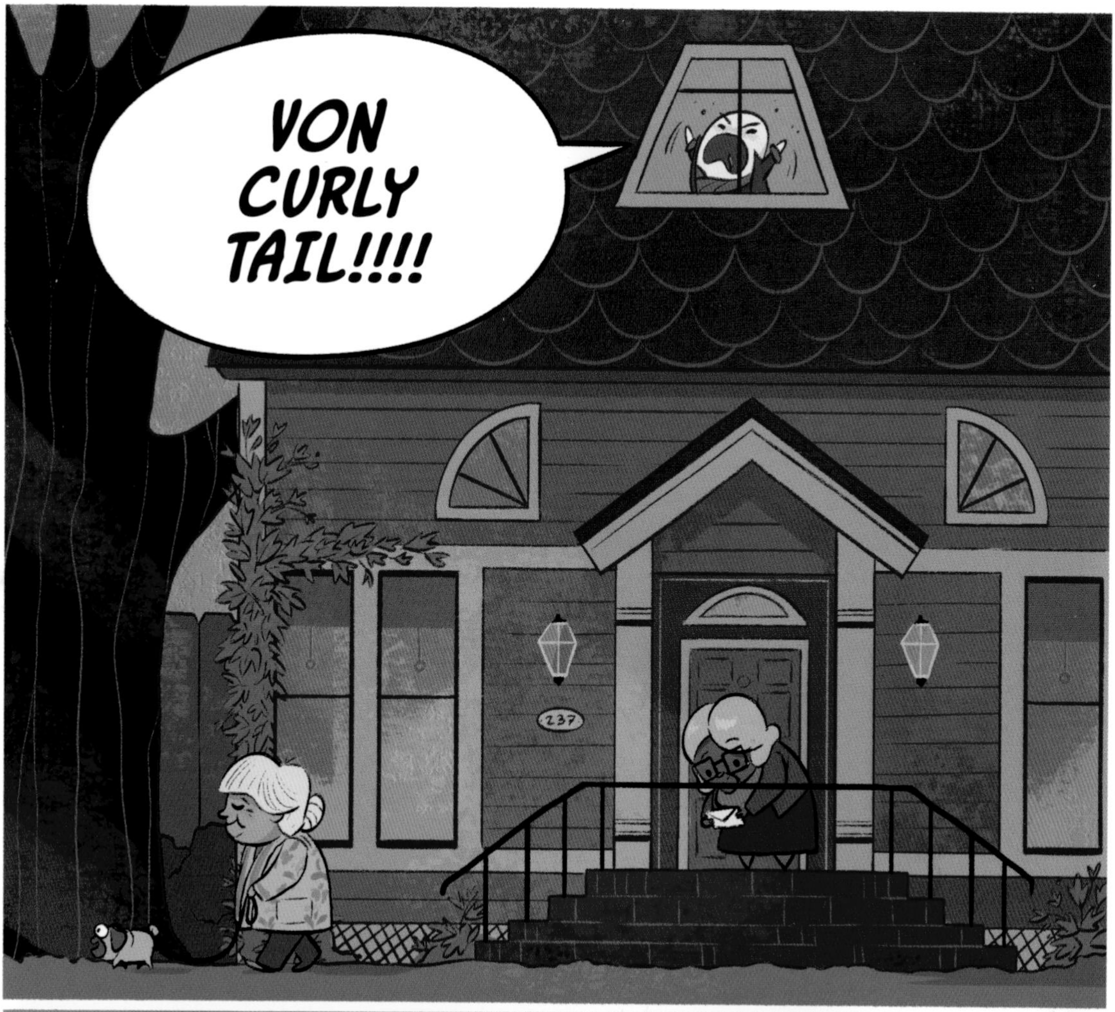
VON CURLY TAIL!!!!
237

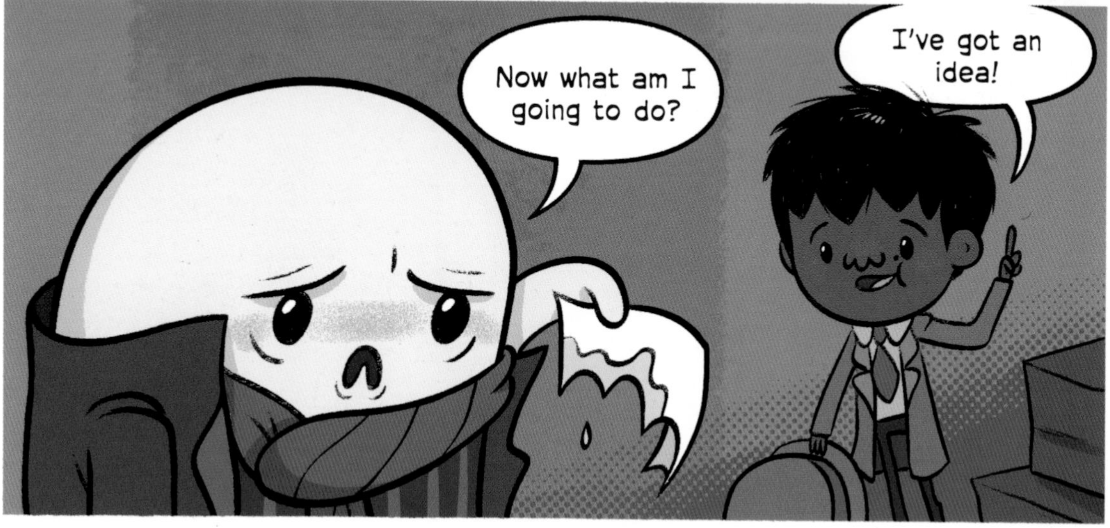
Now what am I going to do?
I've got an idea!

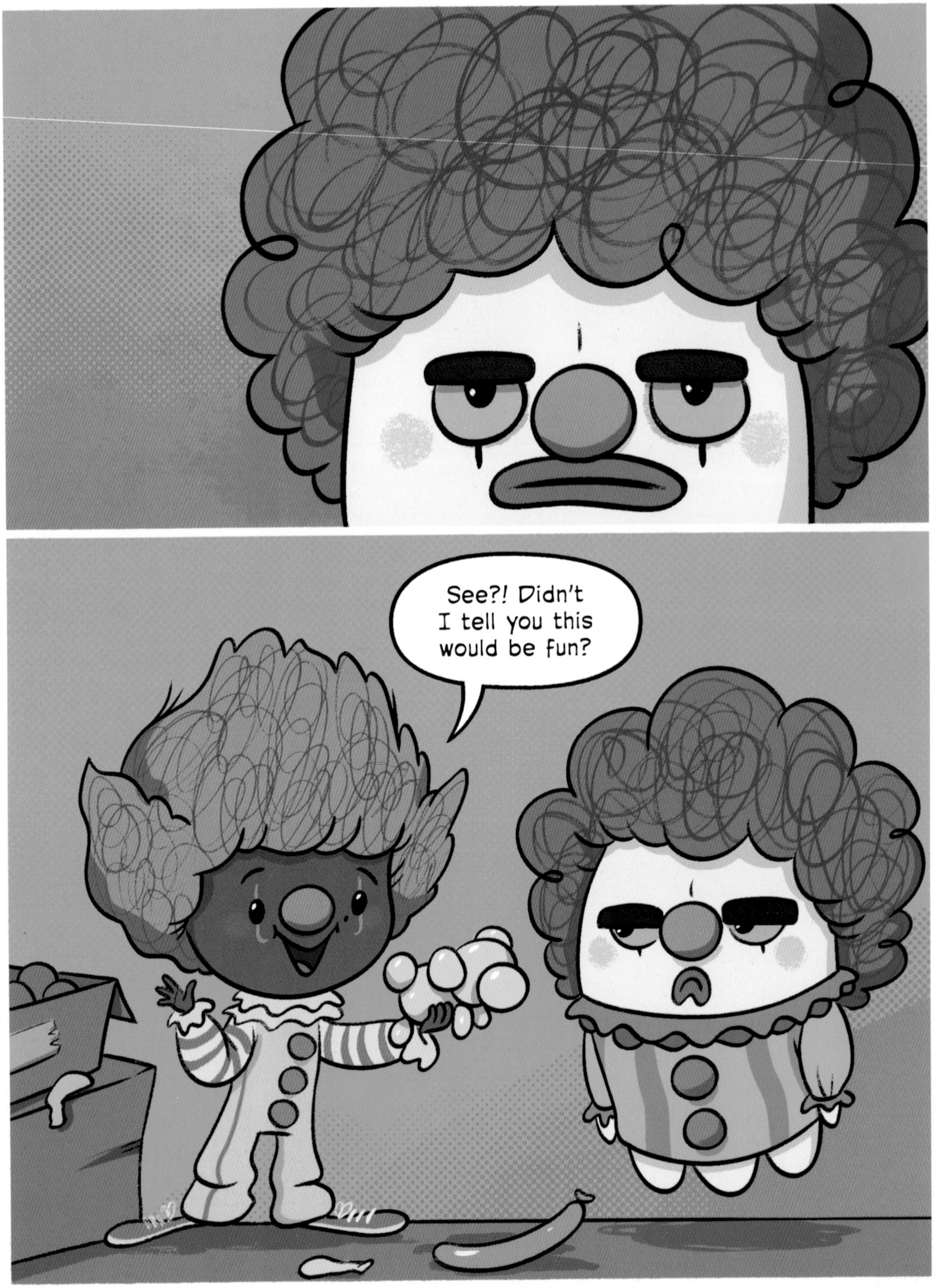
See?! Didn't I tell you this would be fun?